FLANNELWOOD

ALSO BY THE AUTHOR

FICTION
The Last Deaf Club in America
The Kinda Fella I Am
Men with Their Hands

POETRY
A Babble of Objects
The Kiss of Walt Whitman Still on My Lips
How to Kill Poetry
Road Work Ahead
Mute
This Way to the Acorns
St. Michael's Fall

NONFICTION
From Heart into Art:
Interviews with Deaf and Hard of Hearing Artists and Their Allies
Notes of a Deaf Gay Writer: 20 Years Later
Assembly Required: Notes from a Deaf Gay Life

DRAMA
Whispers of a Savage Sort and Other Plays
about the Deaf American Experience
Snooty: A Comedy

AS EDITOR
Lovejets: Queer Male Poets on 200 Years of Walt Whitman
QDA: A Queer Disability Anthology
Among the Leaves: Queer Male Poets on the Midwestern Experience
Eyes of Desire 2: A Deaf GLBT Reader
When I am Dead: The Writings of George M. Teegarden
Eyes of Desire: A Deaf Gay & Lesbian Reader

FLANNELWOOD

a novel

Raymond Luczak

 Red Hen Press | *Pasadena, CA*

Book layout by Mark E. Cull
Cover photograph of Adam Kauwenberg-Marsnik by Raymond Luczak

Library of Congress Cataloging-in-Publication Data

Names: Luczak, Raymond, 1965– author.
Title: Flannelwood : a novel / Raymond Luczak.
Description: First edition. | Pasadena, CA : Red Hen Press, 2019.
Identifiers: LCCN 2018042729 | ISBN 9781597098977
Classification: LCC PS3562.U2554 F58 2019 | DDC 813/.54—dc23
LC record available at https://lccn.loc.gov/2018042729

The National Endowment for the Arts, the Los Angeles County Arts
Commission, the Dwight Stuart Youth Fund, the Max Factor Family
Foundation, the Pasadena Tournament of Roses Foundation, the Pasadena Arts & Culture Commission and the City of Pasadena Cultural Affairs Division, the City of Los Angeles Department of Cultural
Affairs, the Audrey & Sydney Irmas Charitable Foundation, the Ah-
manson Foundation, the Meta & George Rosenberg Foundation, the
Kinder Morgan Foundation, the Allergan Foundation, and the Rior-
dan Foundation all partially support Red Hen Press.

First Edition
Published by Red Hen Press
www.redhen.org

ACKNOWLEDGMENTS

The author wishes to thank Steve Pierson of the Golden Leaf, and Earl Melvin, for their clarifications on the subject matter of cigar smoking. He is grateful to Tom Steele for introducing him to Djuna Barnes's novel *Nightwood* half a lifetime ago. Phillip Herring's definitive biography *Djuna: The Life and Work of Djuna Barnes* makes for worthwhile reading, and *Nightwood: The Original Version and Related Drafts*, edited and with an introduction by Cheryl J. Plumb, has provided helpful insights into the creation of Ms. Barnes's masterwork. He is deeply grateful for the time spent with Peggy Merchak at the VA Hospital going into great detail about the challenges a newly amputated person is likely to confront in rehabilitation. The author appreciates the help and hospitality of Melainie Wilding Garcia, Scott Holl, and John Link. He also appreciates the assistance of Mark Cull, Adam Kauwenberg-Marsnik, and Rebeccah Sanhueza with this book, and the enthusiasm of Kate Gale and Tobi Harper for *Flannelwood*.

for

Anthony Santos

CONTENTS

A man is whole only when he takes into account his shadow.

—*Djuna Barnes*

OF WINTER'S LIGHT I BRING

"I used to think," Nora said, "that people just went to sleep, or if they did not go to sleep that they were themselves, but now"—she lit a cigarette and her hands trembled—"now I see that the night does something to a person's identity, even when asleep."

—*Djuna Barnes*

Your missing right foot was only a part of you, just like the fur that blanketed your body. I remember the look of fear on your face when I'd accidentally opened the bathroom door the morning after we met. You'd just finished showering. I simply needed to piss, but there you were, wet, the many shades of black, gray, and white in your body fur glistening like your beard, and the cone end of your shin. It didn't look real. It wasn't a special effect in a Hollywood movie. What was real was dripping. I saw the crooked scar of brown near the bottom of your shin. It wasn't what I'd thought a limb amputated halfway below the knee would look like in daylight. You'd kept it cloaked, a shroud carrying the unborn child not yours, tucked inside a prosthetic shin and foot. Now it was pink, red, startled with a cry.

I looked up at your face: a volley of fire, spear, armor.

I said, "I'm sorry. I just needed to—"

"Get out." Your whisper rumbled forth at 2,000 decibels. The ice in your voice, jagged and rich, knifed into my eardrums. Surely this would be the end of us. Already before we had our first breakfast, lunch, dinner.

I would've left, but I walked quickly to the stall, where behind you was a shower chair, and knelt before you as you remained standing. I leaned forward to kiss the cone of your shin. I took hold of your beautiful leg and kissed you down there, the space far more private than anywhere else on your body. We had traveled all over the world of each other the night before, but this was uncharted territory. I had to map the rest of your body as you stood petrified, not daring to kick me like the unwelcome conquistador I was. I closed my eyes and kissed the unreal topography of your most private world. I lingered my tongue all over your shin, a brand-new foreign language. I was absolutely frightened of what you would do to me. I didn't know yet how to translate. I'd never been with a disabled man before.

You held onto the wall railing. Your knuckles turned into tiny snowcaps. Your skin dribbled paint drops of clarity. Your body trembled. You weren't erect. I looked up. A glimmer of tears, a gush of aurora borealis. Heaven was marbled in your eyes.

I stood up. "You okay?"

You nodded; looked away. The white tiles in your shower were mirrors in a prison, opaque reflections about to turn full-color bleed.

Even though my body couldn't decide which need was more pressing—ejaculation or urination—I left the bathroom. I could hold it in a few more minutes.

When I saw you again in the kitchen, you were already in your jeans, frying eggs in the cast-iron skillet. You looked up at me with an unexpected softness in your eyes. You had such a stoic face, but here, suddenly you were like an angel about to be given wings, your cocoon molted clear of shoulders, already furred and strapped with muscle. Surely all you had to do was to open up your arms to your full wingspan and take flight.

The way the sunlight rested on your bearded face while we ate . . . *wow*. Oceans once mad with fury came to a still; suddenly a pond filled with cattails and dragonflies in the grays of your eyes. Diamonds of snow married in your eyebrows. The rocks of crag all over the mountainside of your face avalanched into a smile filled with sky. I wanted so much to have my camera right there with me. But you'd made it clear how you disliked having your picture taken. You must've been afraid of disappointing men when they discovered your disability after drinking in one single gulp the hotness of your fur, pecs, cock. If my camera could flit about like a hummingbird, I'd have shot you from below and have you look incredibly imposing, especially if your face and chest were partially covered in shadow.

There's something powerful about shadows. Voices stilled by the dark, voices afraid of the knife of sunlight ready to slash the dark in half, voices afraid to sing.

You weren't just a ghost. You were pure shadow.

That's why you still follow me no matter where I go.

Start anywhere, and there you are.

In my heart, it's always winter.

My heart's trapped inside a snow globe, not just inside the shell of glass, filled almost to the brim just enough to allow a flat bubble of oxygen to push the blanket of faux snow around and about to give the illusion of white falling, but my heart, made of plastic, is glued to a thumb-sized house, an evergreen or two, a frozen pond, two skaters never moving, everything locked to the floor. Shake, shake hard as one usually must, and watch the flakes cascade, settle with a puffy sigh all over the tacky contours, while my heart feels ready to explode from hypothermia. There's not enough furnace. No fire, just room temperature water that will never melt the shellac hardening my heart. I am a child of factory, not of sun nor field, but a spit of souvenir coming down the assembly line.

Sticking a thermometer into the mouth of my heart, under its shivery tongue of flicker and fear, brushing up against the roots of molars, won't help. Made of mercury, the thermometer doesn't register the subzero fickleness of affection; the glass nub, silvery liquid dangerously toxic if broken, swallowed, bleeds dry until I am all glass. Shake me again. Maybe, maybe this time I will crack, a hairline fracture that will splinter the globe into shards, tiny swords that will pierce the cool polish of your heart. I would not rain down but float upward to the heavens where I will regard you, observe all you do, ponder. Go on. Go on, shake me again, and watch me snow tears down my cheeks in the darkness of shellac. Paint my house of heart white. Freeze me until I pale into nothing.

Every night when I lie here on this bed, I dream up conversations that you and I will never have.

Like right now: the window over there by the bed would be wide open, and even in the dead of winter, you'd want to keep it open just a smidge. You hated having a thick blanket on top of you when you slept. You were the kind of guy who felt hot no matter the season. You needed ventilation, wind, flight. Summers were too hot for you even up north. You used to work out for years and gained a lot of muscle until you lost part of your right leg in a car accident one winter evening. The driver was too busy arguing with his wife on his cell phone and hadn't noticed a patch of ice right up ahead by the corner so he couldn't brake his truck hard enough in time to prevent crumpling your side of the car so badly that—well, you couldn't walk so easily like before.

I didn't know all this yet when I saw you the first time at the Eagle on a Friday night. Everyone there seemed to know everyone else, but I didn't know you. Your face, though: not even a discernible expression, a feeling of one way or other; partially hidden by the brim of your baseball cap, so I couldn't see your eyes. I moved to the side for a better look. Your lush beard sang of birch, tall and squat with scarred bark eyeing saplings unweaving from the grass, sparrows twittering about on the telephone lines, balls of dandelion whiskers breaking up from the belly laughs of wind. You sat on a barstool, nursing a drink while Trevor Covins, standing next to you, carried on about something or other with his buddies. A former president of the Browell County Bears, Trevor was a hot daddy with his thick and wiry goatee streaking a bit of gray down the middle of his jaw. He reminded me of certain bears who were damn hot and knew it enough to pose naked long enough to enable nameless strangers like myself with longing upon their natural ruggedness of fur and muscle. I was always paralyzed when he glanced my way. I tried to smile, but he made it clear he wasn't interested in me. I was simply not there, a twig snapped in half and rolled off the sidewalk.

That's why I didn't look at you again, even though you were woofy as hell. Your T-shirt, pulled on so tight, showed nipples pushing against the fabric. Your forearms were densely coated with fur that shimmered like rubies from the neon behind you. Your black beard was thick with gray and white unbraiding its strands everywhere, ropes of ship fraying at last from too many nights of storms at sea. Then you smiled slightly at someone in my direction. I glanced around, unsure if you'd smiled at me. No one was standing right next to me. No one was looking back at you, or me, or had someone been there, in that moment of my head turning to look, or had I imagined you looking my way at all? When I returned to you, it was as if I wasn't there, no longer a blip on your radar.

James, look at me. In bear parlance, I'm considered a cub even though I don't see myself that way at all. I'm forty-five years old, five feet nine, and 197 pounds with a scruffy beard. I don't work out much. I'm gaining a bit of permanent weight every year, but I'm okay with that. I've always liked guys with a bit of padding on their bones, but not too much. I've never liked those anorexic twinks with haircuts so gelled that they looked like pewter under a mirror ball. During the nineties I saw those images of men dying of AIDS, skinny and laced with pockmarks of pallor. Their teeth sometimes reminded me of Max Schreck's in *Nosferatu*. They were so young, so ravaged, and yet used for inspiration the same way disabled kids were used on Jerry Lewis's Labor Day telethons back in the seventies. Seeing those men's faces, weakened hands taped and wired with IV tubes designed to sell bravery—and newspapers and magazines, too, as they'd understood how

Americans liked to gawk in the perpetual museum of freedom and horror—made each kiss I got from a man feel like charcoal skin—my own!—ready to crumble from the merest kiss of air. I wasn't heavy back then. I knew I liked stocky guys, but I didn't know about the bear community. It seems so obvious now, but I didn't know where I could find *gay* stocky guys. I went out to the bars and clubs near the university, which were filled with young college guys like myself. They wanted to dance and party all night long, and they wanted to stagger, drunk and horny, with someone they barely knew, back to their dorm rooms. They didn't want to think of dense textbooks, exams, grades; they'd become sloppily researched textbooks on love's woes, having waxed and waned, and still didn't learn a damn thing. They never took the time to study themselves in action, become case studies in the mirror of alcohol and haze of smoke, conduct experiments with tighter controls. Their hearts turned into footnotes of woe gone weary, now wary from age. Today they just fudge their stats when they cruise online for another hookup.

I never drank. Just never liked the taste of alcohol. Beer makes me feel queasy, like after ten loop-de-loops on the rollercoaster right after another without stopping, so I'm always someone's designated driver. I never minded. I like seeing things clearly.

Funny how I hadn't seen you so clearly until recently. I am a rearview mirror, sailing through space as your car careened out of control across the slickness of ice.

Hello guys!

I'm on this site because I think bearish men who aren't afraid of oil and grease are mighty fine. I don't use moisturizers or get pedicures either. I like my men to be of the rough and tumble variety. Shirts that show off your round pecs and bellies can be just as hot as fur that shoots out of collars.

If you spend your free time on video games, we are not a match.

If you are comfortable with long sentences, stick around. You won't be disappointed. I promise not to bore you with the same old, same old.

If you think my profile is too long, please click elsewhere for your next victim.

Please don't ask for my X-rated pictures. I don't have any. Sorry about that, fellas.

I'm a former farm boy who's an overworked and underpaid barista at the corner of Broadway and Hancock. You know that place, and I'm sure I've seen at least half of you ask for a cuppa caw-fee. If you see me again, be sure to say hello and give me a special wink (woofs are always welcomed) so I know you're a member of our bear family. ;-)

For those who are wondering about my stats, I just turned 45 (how the hell did that happen?!?), 5'9" (taller if I wear platform shoes, but I lost them one wicked Halloween), and 194 lbs (I keep trying to lose weight all the time, but if you can accept the fact that I may never be svelte again, that's a big plus).

If I'm not busy watching movies that require a little brain-power to digest (like subtitles), I'm always reading. A good book is always like a good friend you wish you had. It's like having a great conversation you wish more people would have. At any given time, I'm usually jump-reading two or three books. Right now I'm reading Cheryl Strayed's WILD (was she really that ill-prepared for a long hike?), Jeanette Winterson's WRITTEN ON THE BODY (definitely one of her best), and Nicholson Baker's THE ANTHOLOGIST (a funny story about a man who tries so hard to write a foreword to an anthology but just can't). Of course I have many favorite books, so let's chat.

A singer that I wish more people knew about is Drake Jensen. I don't much care for country music, but have you ever seen him? He's friggin' HOT. And no, he's not a closet case. You should check him out in the music video "Fast Enough for Me." His voice is sexy fine. I wish he'd croon to me naked. His hubba-bubba is sure a lucky fella.

If you've gotten this far, congratulations. It means your attention span is long enough to hold a conversation in person. If you like to talk about the arts, that's a plus too.

But if you still feel overwhelmed, relax. I'm actually an easygoing sweetheart. Let's give ourselves a whirl of chitchat over a scoop or two at Cold & N'ice. Who knows, you might be lucky to find out what a great romp I am in the bedroom. Date is not a four-letter word.

Looking forward to hearing from ya.

Thanks, guys!

Bill

LAST UPDATED ON SEPT 23, 2013

James.

James. Oh, God. The way you light me up at night when I least expect it.

James. I whisper your name in the dark and watch it catch fire on the wind, tiny little flickers flouncing in the air that no one ever notices because their eyes are on the ground where they walk. The tiny curls of smoke dance and unfurl like wisps of hair just pruned, falling in tender clumps around the barber's chair. Everything is ether and then some.

James. Your name means "supplanter." You supersede and replace; old plants pulled out of the soil, new seeds sown. You have vision. The future is already in your rearview mirror. You take over the past, remake it as your own. The land is rooted deep inside your bones, musty earth damp from flash rains. You didn't like it when people tried to call you Jim or Jimmy. You were quiet but firm about your name. You were to be addressed as James. Your shadow on the ground was sharp as blades.

James Alan. Your middle name means "handsome." The stars poured the sugar of beauty deep into your veins and the moon peppered your skin with salt, and the skies pumped your eyes with blue and the clouds filled the rest of you with ocean, limitless as the horizon on an overcast day, so your body was of this earth and sea, your cock stripped bare at low tide, your past hidden at high tide. There was never an in-between, a landing with you; just a fleeting glance, a grip of slippery hands, a call for help, a plea from deep in the forest for a little understanding, a tenderness. But how you've lingered in the coral reef of my tongue, a breeze of balm floating just so, oh just *so* in my nose.

James Alan Sutton. You are the fire in the chimney of my soul. How I keep crackling, wood splintering amidst splotches of ember, singeing. I am nothing without winter's ache. In the polar vortex of my heart, you hold all my matches.

On the first day of spring, you called me at the coffeehouse out of the blue. I was on a break.

"Hey."

"Oh, hi, James!" I was surprised. It was a Thursday, and you always called me on Friday morning to confirm that I was indeed available to go up north for the weekend. "What's up?"

"Okay." A pause. "Look, I've been doing some thinking. Um, I've been thinking that maybe this is not gonna work." I could hear in the background the faint hum of factory where you worked.

"What? We've been spending weekends together for—"

"Sorry," you said. "I just don't think we're a good fit."

"Wait. I don't understand. I thought things were going great. Six months. Hello?"

"Look," you said. "You want what I can't give."

"What's that?"

"You want a boyfriend and all of that."

"What's wrong with wanting all of that?"

"It's not you. It's me."

"Look," I said. "Shouldn't we, um, talk about this in person? I mean—"

"Gotta go. Sorry."

Click.

That turned out to be our last conversation.

I left a ton of voicemails, but you didn't answer.

March 20, 2014 was the first day of winter in my heart.

Sometimes I wish you could come into the room of my dreams and sit down on the sofa over there. Let my memory play its accordion, snippets of song we'd overheard while talking with each other in your truck, the unexpected pats on the shoulder, the ferocity of tongue into the darkest caverns of each other. We are the paintings in the Cave of El Castillo, we are the learned of Mesopotamia, and what's left of us are the myths that will never abandon us no matter how long we shiver in the rain.

Listen not to the sound of rain beating down on the tin roof above us, but to the music of letting go from the hands of clouds once cupping so much water, so many tears. In that blind drop to earth, we awaken just long enough to see the grass ready to impale us a half-second before we hit and disintegrate into mist. Realign the radio antennae of ear to my broadcasts of everything about us. Television, and online too.

There, on my battered sofa in the opulent room of my dreams, you would slowly dawn upon me and fill me with the sunlight of your soul. Rain gone, long gone, you would stand up, the gentle giant that you are, and look down into my eyes. You'd say, "Come with me."

I'd float right beside you.

We wouldn't have the need to discuss anything; telepathy would be sufficient.

In that grotto where you liked to smoke a cigar alone, it would be perennially summer, and it would be there where you would marry me. We would be together until the time came for us to let go. At a hundred and one years of age, you would be the grizzled oak of a man, and I would be resting my head, the eternal sapling that I am, on your chest where I could hear the last of your heart-beat fade into eternity.

I would die happily a few moments later.

We would be buried together in the same cemetery plot, and our tombstone would read, TWO MEN HERE HAVE LOVED EACH OTHER LIKE NO TWO EVER HAVE. No names or years lived and died. Leave behind the most mysterious story for others to imagine and write. Love is a ghost that, once infected, never dies. It remains fatal and incurable. It haunts every bed we sleep in until the day we die.

You haunt me still.

Not knowing what one's done wrong is the quickest way to become a ghost. Regrets are what make us lose skin, soul, control. We become bound to sins we are never quite sure if we've committed. We become filled with doubts that weigh down on our shoulders. We are sinners accursed with the sentence of uncertainty, so we haunt and haunt until we learn the answers. By then we've turned ourselves into ghosts, and it's too late to change our ways. It's much easier to flail in a sea of familiar pain than to soar like an albatross in the terrifying sky.

Should I continue and try to solve the mystery of you, or would you be one of those nasty corpses, found tossed into a ditch, that offers no clue as to why you'd died?

Have I fallen for a ghost who didn't know he'd died long before he'd met me?

Are you a specter accursed with cold blood?

Do you remember how we first met? I even remember the date: Friday, October 4, 2013.

When I saw you again for the second time, it was at the annual OctoBear Dance held at the VFW Hall on Portland Avenue. By then I'd searched all the local profiles for you on Bear411, and there you were. Someone had snapped a picture of you leaning against a stucco wall. Your arm rested on something out of frame, but there was something deep in your eyes. You had seen a lot of things you wished you hadn't seen. You wore an old denim shirt, which you'd left open a bit at the top. The denseness of your chest fur mesmerized me. I figured you to be in your mid-fifties.

In the VFW Hall, you sat alone at a table away from the make-shift stage. The music was loud, even with only two speakers out by the stage; the husky DJ, who had a flaming red beard, had a notorious reputation for sleeping with the new arrivals before any-one else in the community did. I'm proud to say that he'd failed with me. I talked with some of my buddies near the doors that opened to the main hall where the music wasn't too bad, but I couldn't take my eyes off you the whole time. How could such an insanely hot stud be sitting all by himself? Where were your friends? I saw Trevor holding forth with his buddies, all muscu-lar and good-looking. They were busy laughing and drinking beer from their plastic cups. I felt angry. Had they brushed you off with attitude? I didn't know what to do. Should I even say hello to you?

When I saw Trevor glance your way and break into a laugh while cracking a joke, I knew what I had to do. I walked over there to your table. I was petrified that you'd give me attitude like your buddies, but I tripped against a chair leg jutting out and nearly hit your table with my forehead. I knelt halfway under the table.

"Hey, you all right?"

I looked across to your legs to check out your ample crotch, because hey, I'm a guy, right? I scanned down your legs. Wait—your right foot didn't have an ankle inside your black sneakers. It was shiny like aluminum. Then I realized that you were wearing a prosthetic foot. Had to be. Then I checked out your ample crotch again, because hey, I'm a guy, right?

I pushed myself up onto my feet. "Yeah." I felt a bit shaky, but I didn't want you to see that. You see, I didn't know what to think when I saw your missing foot. All I knew was that I had found you to be sexy, but that . . .

"You sure?"

"Uh, yes."

"Why don't you sit down?"

A blush of shame and embarrassment seeped into my face. I felt like a schoolboy sitting in front of his principal in his office, waiting to be sentenced to after-school detention. I didn't dare look into your eyes.

"Hey."

"I'm sorry. What?"

"Are you freaking out over my foot?"

"Yes." I didn't look up.

"I'd still freak out, but what choice do I have? Either I stay home and feel sorry for myself, or I put myself out there and hope for the best." He extended his hand into my line of vision. "Hello?"

I had been staring at your huge hand. Thick strands of fur lined the back of your fingers. I think I involuntarily licked my own lips. I felt skittish when I shook your hand for the first time.

"Name's James."

"I'm Bill Badamore."

"Nice to meet you, Bill."

"Likewise."

"Don't be scared of me. I don't bite, and my missing foot ain't contagious. I'm not a zombie."

"Right. Right."

"It's okay." You took my hand and squeezed it; I nearly creamed in my pants. I was that stiff. I wanted to rub my face all over your furry chest.

"Well, if I knew about your . . ."

"Disability. It's not a dirty word. It just is."

"Sorry."

"Don't be." You smiled. "You're very cute. My very able-bodied friend between my legs thinks so too." My face must've been quite crimson because you grinned broadly at me. "Did you come here with your car?"

"Actually, I walked here. I live fifteen blocks from here."

"Do you . . . uh, wanna play? I live an hour north of here. You'd have to stay the night. You okay with that?"

If I were a character in a cartoon, my jaw would've hit the floor.

You smiled. "Why don't I meet you outside by the parking lot in ten minutes?"

I nodded.

"You go right ahead. I have to go to the restroom first."

I got up and felt light as a dream. You weren't just a hot face in a hookup app, a picture of hotness that gets reposted all over Tumblr. As I walked to the coat check and picked up my flannel-lined denim jacket, I was so afraid to look back at you; I wondered how you'd move with that fake foot. Okay, okay: I admit it. I was afraid of being seen with you, limping along while going out of that place together, but I didn't check back on you. I was afraid that everyone would think that I was into having sex with freaks. I was relieved that you needed to go to the bathroom anyway. I waited outside in the parking lot and wondered if you were for real. It had been a lifetime since a stranger had met me in person and asked me to his home.

Outside you walked naturally in and out of street-lit shadows toward me. I was surprised you weren't limping! You looked made of night in your leather jacket. I hadn't realized just how tall you were. You told me later that you were six-five. Had I conjured you out of thin air?

"Hey." There was a sadness in your eyes. "You're scared of me, right?"

"No. I mean, I don't know. I've never—"

In that moment you grabbed the back of my head and brought my lips to yours. You kissed me, and it was as if a dust-covered light bulb deep inside me went on. If I had felt skittish before, I wasn't anymore.

I kissed you right back.

"Oh, you're easy," you responded with a light laugh.

I followed you to your truck, which was clean. No bits of garbage on the floor. For some reason I'd thought you would have a 4x4 Jeep, but your truck was retrofitted with an additional arm stick to take the place of your missing foot. I felt strange sitting next to you. All I could do was to look at your visage flickering in the passing lights of neon and traffic as we coasted out of the city.

I wanted to make conversation, but I was afraid of sounding too smart-alecky and scaring you away.

You smiled at me. "Hey."

"What?"

"I've seen you talk with your friends at the dance, so . . ."

"Sorry. I don't know what to say."

"I'm tired of the radio. Tell me about yourself."

"Well, what do you want to know?"

"Anything. We got fifty minutes left."

That's how I ended up telling you about my devout Catholic family. I have one sister and three brothers, who have this strange idea that all gay people are pedophiles hell-bent on fondling kids. That's why I haven't seen them for a long time. It's hard because I've grown up with them, and when I'm honest with them, they don't want me. Did that mean they didn't love me enough? My mother died when I was twenty-eight. My family votes Republican because they don't feel that gay people deserve "special rights." Never mind the fact that we gay people simply want the same rights they have. The phrase "special rights" is pure homophobia.

You were quiet the whole time. Your eyes stayed steady on the road, and the green lights from the dashboard lit your face. With the way shadows played on your face, you looked as if you were half-ghost, half-human; you glowed radiation. In the flickering darkness I couldn't read your face. I didn't know what you'd thought of me. Had I said too much?

I stopped talking.

"You okay?"

"I think I said too much. Politics is such a downer anyway."

"It's okay. I like learning about you, and what you've said, I like it very much."

"Really?"

"Yes. Go on."

I talked about working as a barista-slash-assistant manager for what people consider a "chic" coffeehouse, but happens to be as generic and corporate as any fast food chain. Brewe Sisters is actually a Starbucks wannabe. I rattled off the popular coffee blends I make every day. I swore that it was not a joke when customers gave very specific instructions for their coffees. At first it was very confusing to keep things straight, but like anything else, repetition would make everything easy to do. I had wanted to become a writer, but having a MFA in Creative Writing doesn't have much cred if you don't have a lot of things published. I'd always wanted to become a poet, but no one wanted my poems. I think I got into my MFA program on the *promise* of my work sample and my undergraduate GPA of 4.0, but I can't say that I'm as talented as people seem to think. Every day at the coffee shop I see people sit at the tiny tables with their laptops, and they seem to be able to write in spite of the distractions all around them. I envy them. I've always wanted to write a novel, but I'm too easily distracted. Plus there's no money in literary fiction, which is what I want to do. I want to tell stories that explore what it means to be human, to be part of the world, blah blah blah. I don't care too much for genre fiction. Not sure why. Maybe it feels so formulaic. Since I make pitiful income from my job, I borrow books from the library all the time. I say I'm a writer, but I've given up on writing. Just not worth it.

You said, "You don't have to give up. You're still young enough."

"Oh, please. I'm forty-five."

Then I asked you about your life.

You told me you worked in a food processing plant, prepping beets for canning. You dropped out of community college when you got a woman pregnant. You stayed married for three years, and you started having sex with guys in public restrooms. You were so scared of getting caught, but you met this guy Jeff in one of them. Turned out that he was married with kids just like you, and you two weren't happy with your wives, so you told your wife that you met someone else. She never stopped giving you hell for the next fifteen years. You gave her full custody of your daughter, and you paid alimony and child support. You longed to see your daughter, Annie, more often, but she was basically a stranger to you until the day she came back from Houston, divorced and pregnant at thirty-one. She wept in your arms. You had to tell her that you didn't have room for her and her kid in your small house. By then, you and Jeff had been broken up for a long time. He moved to the burbs southwest of the city, where he worked at a sewage plant. He was too heartbroken when his ex-wife remarried and moved to Florida. Of course, she took the kids with her. He hated feeling like a stranger to his kids so he too relocated there. You still hear from him time to time. You just can't bear the idea of living too close to a city where people are rude to each other. Too noisy, too crowded, too expensive. You liked working in the plant, where you've been for the last thirty-seven years. Your coworkers were loyal to you. Your boss had said that your missing foot was enough grounds for dismissal due to potential safety issues, but everyone rallied around you. You just can't imagine working anywhere else, and you've been saving up for your retirement. But it's been difficult at times when a good prosthetic limb and foot could be as expensive as a new car. You talked a lot about wanting to become a woodworker in your garage once you retired.

I never thought you'd turn silent on the subject of your past after that first night.

I didn't notice it at first, but when we made love that first night, you kept the bottom half of your right leg hidden. You hadn't taken your jeans all the way off. When I went down on you, I rubbed my hands all over your thighs and knees, and without thinking, I moved my hands below the knees to continue rubbing the rest of your legs through the jeans. I felt jarred when I felt the brace holding your prosthetic foot. This of course hiccupped the rhythm of my cocksucking, but I averted my eyes from yours. My tongue resumed its loving. You never said a word about my tongue *interruptus*. Even after having orgasmed twice already together that night, I couldn't risk asking you about your missing foot. I was afraid of breaking the trance-like atmosphere we were both in. Finally, you whispered, "We need to stop." You smiled. "For now."

It was so beautiful to see that light in your eyes. Do you know how rare it was to be seen with such eyes full of tenderness and warmth as in that moment? I don't know how you'd loved the other guys in your past, but I know how special I'd felt in your arms. I made sure to sleep on your left side so that if I curled my legs around you, I wouldn't embarrass you by reminding you of your phantom foot. Did you ever notice that?

You pulled up your jeans, went to the bathroom, and turned out the lights when you returned. I felt you pull off your jeans and your prosthetic foot. Thinking of you taking off your foot like a person taking off his shoes before going to bed was a weird concept.

In the dark you explained to me that you didn't mind cuddling for a short period of time, but you required space for sleep. After closing my eyes and feeling the intense warmth of your body, I immediately understood why you preferred not to cuddle. You were like a furnace! You turned to your side, facing the window, and I lay on my back, glancing at your massive silhouette. I was so drained that I managed to fall asleep, even in an unfamiliar bed.

In my high school, there were two groups of smokers. The rich kids had to show how cool they were next to their shiny cars, and the ne'er-do-wells somehow had the money for cigarettes. The rich kids hung out in the parking lot, and the scrappy kids stood mostly hidden in the alley across the street from the school. The school administrators turned a blind eye though they stressed the dangers of smoking in their health ed classes.

What I remember most from those classes was how negative everything was. If you were to have sex, you had to think about condoms or you'd get someone pregnant or get AIDS. If you had to drink, you had to think about not driving. If you did marijuana, you could get arrested and worse. Not once did anyone mention that sex could be so wonderful.

Until I met my first boyfriend, I was furtive with sex, even oral sex. I was skittish, afraid that I was going to get *it*. He said, "Take your time. I'm not going anywhere."

I examined his body to my heart's content, and I came to feel better about my own body. He gave me the confidence I needed.

Then I saw your body, and I felt like a child again. How could my body compete with the majestic sculpture that was your body? You stood tall like an equestrian statue in a park. You were a redwood tree in bas-relief. You moved slowly and surely. Didn't matter if you were wearing a prosthetic foot or not, you were surefooted.

It's not every day that I meet a veritable god, let alone sleep with him. I gave up on organized religion a long time ago, but until I met you, I never understood the meaning of the word "worship." With you, I exhaled wonder.

I didn't fall in love with you our first night together. I'd been around the block enough times to know that what we had experienced was a case of acute lust. I was afraid to hope that you'd want an encore, or that you didn't want a relationship, or anything to do with me again. I didn't want to jinx us.

Imagine how I felt when you asked me to stay another night. We had spent the afternoon naked in your living room. We watched an old Carole Lombard film on the Turner Classic Movies channel. I'd never seen it before. I thought she was a bit screechy in parts, but you had definitely acquired a taste for her. The other night I happened to see *My Man Godfrey* on TV at my house. It was the only time in my life when I laughed and cried at the same time. I wanted to be Lombard's Irene to your Godfrey. The idea of an amputee butler hopping about serving drinks was ridiculous for he would be sure to lose a drop. But of course, you wouldn't. You possessed more grace inherently than in any man I'd met.

I'll always think of you as My Man James.

In the dark of night, when our bodies first became acquainted with each other, I saw the chest-wide tattoo on your back. Blue-black feathers had been artfully arranged to look like wings so that when you lifted your arms, it looked as if you were about to take flight. The fur coating your feathers made it more lifelike. Were you truly an abandoned creature not of this earth? In that moment of seeing your naked body with your massive wings and meaty ass, I felt honored to be in your presence. You'd made it clear that you didn't see yourself as a god, but if only we could fly, the strata of puffy mist would've been sweet to us, buffering the hiccups of our flying in between the holy annunciations of orgasm. You wouldn't have been ashamed of your imperfect leg; I wouldn't be ashamed of my flat pecs and growing flab. Together we would've inspired hope in the hearts of those down on their luck with love.

On our last day together, although I didn't know it then, you surprised me. Just before it was time for us to leave your house for our ride back to the city, you turned around before opening the door to the outside and pulled me into your arms. It was strange to feel the mass of your body, not naked, through the stiff layer of your leather jacket atop the clothes inside. Your hug was fierce, hard. I thought you'd squeeze the air out of me, but I didn't resist. This was the expected moment, long overdue, when you'd admit that you loved me. "Thanks." There was a slight tremor in your voice.

"For what?"

"I feel like such an ass sometimes. I'm not very good about thanking people."

"I'm always thankful for every weekend with you."

"Well." You smiled briefly and kissed me lightly on the lips. "Should we go?"

Our conversation on the way back to my house was light, breezy. We talked about movies. Nothing heavy. It was as if we were meant to be, and this we would continue.

Just when I was about to get out of the truck in front of my house, you patted my knee. "See ya."

I waved good-bye, and you were gone.

Until then, and not even then, at least not until you hung up on me, did I understand what it meant to miss someone, not just a first love, but someone who'd made me feel alive more than anyone else.

You I miss I miss you I miss: my heart doesn't know how to speak coherently anymore.

That familiar feeling of anticipation steamrolls me every Friday evening, and I get sideswiped when I remember you haven't called me to confirm.

The first few Fridays after you hung up on me I brought in my weekend bag to work, hoping that you'd change your mind at the last minute and give me a call as if nothing had happened. I kept looking out the window all day long.

I tried to read a book on those Friday nights, but I couldn't focus. I simply had to close my eyes and have another dream conversation with you while I listened to music in the heaven of my ear buds.

I still think of you reclining on your side in the twilight between evening and dawn. I couldn't see your face at all; just your Mount Rushmore backside. The absence of your face, always a treasure trove of clues, has made you too much of a mystery.

When you first hung up on me, I thought it was your way of say-ing that, if not a new guy in your life, you'd been diagnosed with a fatal disease, like cancer. You knew how hard it had been for me to watch my first boyfriend fade away into a frightening heap of splotches and joints with barely a face. Maybe you wanted the redwood tree of you to shrink back into the broken sapling you must've felt yourself to be. I longed to tell you that I'd do it all over again with Craig, right down to his last moment, only that I would constantly tell him how much I loved him, show him how much by holding him like the child I felt like when he was strong and healthy in loving me in the days before he became sick. I'd have done the same for you.

One night I dreamed of coasting down from the clouds above the ocean and seeing you there inside a glass coffin. I could see the nakedness of you, your arms bowed across your chest, as you looked peaceful in the sun shining. The sea around you had no horizon, and I was the lone seagull holding easily in the same spot above you, looking down on you. The winds kept me aloft as I fol-lowed your coffin bobbing gently in the waves. Hours dragged on with the sun not leaving. Ever. There was no night. Death stayed all day. The sun bored down long enough through the glass top of your coffin right at your face until your body caught fire and filled the coffin with smoke. I swooped down and tried to peck at the glass top with my beak, but I wasn't strong enough. I couldn't stay long on the coffin; the heat from the fire within was too intense for my webbed feet. I tried to propel upward onto the winds that had kept me floating easily, but the waves were gone. No wind.

I pushed off your coffin onto the water.

I tucked in my wings and floated around your coffin. I paddled back and forth. My motions were the start of a huge wave that I didn't see coming from behind until it was too late. The tiny old me had caused a tsunami made of fury and tenderness, but I didn't see it coming. I was that focused on the fissures of smoke seeping through the fractures of your glass coffin. The cracks splintered into tiny islands that floated away from us, glittering like fat diamonds in the sun, and then the bottom of your coffin gave way. Your body, having been embalmed with the toxins of lies and love, had melted into goo.

The most horrible darkness rose above me, and—

Something—a huge hand? a slosh of wave?—slapped my frail body hard, far, far into the distance, I was flung so quickly, so hard, it felt as if my feathers would be plucked from velocity, as the dark tall waves chilled and ice-cubed everything. Everything that the waves had touched got the loud kissquake of death and turned into the Death Valley of ice. The force of my flight was such that I sailed straight across, not down, until the globe slid underneath me and I saw the faint silhouette of a mountain—no, an island. The mountain jutted so high up in the clouds that it was easy for me to swerve my tired wings to the right and coast down to the shore. The water around the island was warm. I made myself at home under a coconut tree and went straight to sleep.

At that moment I woke up in my bed. I didn't want to forget you. Not now, not ever.

Please don't die. You are not something once beautiful found in an ocean. The world is full of bottled elegies waiting to be opened and heard.

Inhaling you deeply after a week of imbibing the myriad smells of coffee at work was a much-needed heaven of musk. You had worked all day, moving up and down the assembly line doing quality checks and troubleshooting; you had twenty-six people working for you. You never showered right after work when you came down to the city and picked me up, so your truck was perfumed with the Chanel No. 5 of sweat, the most sublime odor much like the fresh break of soil the morning after a night of deep rain, the kind that reminds me of moss and mushrooms, the taste of you unfiltered, unlike a cigarette, filling my nose and tongue until the aroma, pungent like men's rooms and lusty like gyms, leaped down my esophagus and into the capillaries of my veins until my entire body became a single pump of blood coalescing into the trunk of my cocktree, glistening with the resin of desire. I groveled happily like a pig sniffing furiously for that hidden gold of truffle lost in the roots of your armpits. I swallowed your pearl-seeds deep into the lining of my stomach, a fallow field waiting to be sowed. I floated, a spore of mushroom amber whispering on the wind of your breath.

Come shade me with the beads of rain from your eyebrows. I am fungi, and you are bark. Together we will burrow roots deep into the earth and never bury our history.

When you first asked me to stay with you on weekends, I felt giddy. There had been many moments in my life after college that made me wonder if anybody wanted to date. Seriously. Didn't matter if their profiles had said that they were looking for a long-term relationship. Guys simply don't want to date. They say that they want to date and possibly have a LTR, but that's just a come-on to guys who don't sleep around. They're fresh meat. That's what I'd learned from online dating, which is why I don't pay attention whenever someone says in his profile that he's interested in dating. Not true.

Each weekend up north with you felt like some sort of test. The problem was, I never knew what kind of test I was supposed to pass.

In our first hour together in your truck, I kept looking at your dashboard-lit face. We talked like shadows skirting the halo of light.

You slowed the truck down. I hadn't realized that we were already close to your house. The road we were on had been lonely with no traffic. Up ahead was a small white house with a sconce lamp next to the door. We got out of your truck. In the distance,

I could hear an owl *whoo*ing. The stars were clear above us. The October air was crisp. "Come on," you said.

I walked around the front of your truck, and you grabbed my arm. You pulled me close. Your tongue on my lips demanded attention. You gripped your arms around me, and I couldn't stop roaming my hands all over your back, your firm ass. You were strong as soil, land. Everything was a crisp quiet, yet a million little sounds surrounded us. I couldn't pinpoint anything, but they were loud. I had no idea! But I loved the feeling of muscle tensed up in your back. You had worked your body for a long, long time. Even if you seemed like a big guy with a flat belly, you had very little fat. I loved looking up into your face. Something about guys taller than me gets my engine humming happily.

Finally you panted. "Let's get inside."

Your house was small and well-maintained. Nothing was ever out of place. The checkered linoleum floor in the kitchen showed its age, but everything else was clean. There was a nook with a built-in table off to the side, like a booth in a diner. The gas stove was small. The lights above were fluorescent, but soon warmed up to a more pleasant glow.

You took my hand and led me straight down the hall to your bedroom. I was struck by the fact that the hallway didn't have pictures hung on the walls. Then I saw on the wood paneling the softened scuffs from hands having touched the walls too often. In the tiny bedroom you leaned against a tall dresser for a brief moment before you took off your T-shirt. I gasped. I'd never seen such dense fur up close. I had seen many pictures of furry chests online, but nothing prepared me for the vision of you. This time I pulled you into my arms. My fingers felt alive feeling those thick strands of you weaving in and out of them. I gasped again when I felt the fur on your back. I felt as if I'd found manna. Indeed your body was the closest to heaven I've ever experienced here on earth.

You said, "Take off your shirt, boy."

I cringed at being called "boy." I know that when a man is older, the younger one is usually called "boy," or sometimes "son." But
I wasn't looking for a daddy. I was so boned up that I didn't correct
you. I simply pulled off my T-shirt. I was afraid that you'd find my
body not to your liking.

Your hands rubbed all over my hairless back. The first time you
have sex with someone can be haphazard. You don't know yet the
exact locations of his erogenous zones or what else turns him on.
You two stumble blindly at times around each other in the heat
of fearing that this one time together will be the only time you'll
ever have together. You find that one guy likes to have his nipples
pulled up hard, and another guy can't stand it because his nipples
are too sensitive. And so on. I find that the second and third times
with the same guy are always better. I know to zero right in on
what turns him on. It's great having sex with the same guy over
and over again.

I remember thinking the same thought about you when our
hands and tongues and mouths and bodies fell into contact. We
were magnets that couldn't be pulled apart. Don't you remember
that? I do. My body still does.

Allow me to stand here in the Great Hall of Soldiers, graced with
marble and memory, if you will please, kind sir, so I may swear my
oath of loyalty to you before all.

Let me be your soldier of love.

Let my hands visit the landmarks of pain embedded in your
body.

Let them drill deep for the crude oil of release and relief so that
you will see only gold in your feelings.

Let them map the land mines of self-control hidden in your
body so you can trip them safely without losing another foot.

Let them operate on your wounded heart and let the steady
drip of blood from my heart transfuse and blend into yours.

Let me be your liberator.

Let the war inside you be over. It's gone on for too long. When love's the object of war, no one wins. The prize is only a country of hurt.

Let me prove my undying allegiance to the most magnificent country of you.

When I was a kid, I loved looking out on the snow-swept fields at night. The moon gave them a cool glow, and if I squinted just so, I could see diamonds littering the white dunes. The trees were black as silhouettes. No fine details anywhere. They had been deadened, broad-stroked into iconic symbols.

After you hung up on me, I thought of you wearing a long cape that flowed behind you in the subzero winds. Your beard was as long as a wedding dress train, and it was beautiful to behold. It shifted shape like a cat's tail, yet not as slender. It caught the wind of your emotions as you plodded with your crutches. It wasn't clear where you were headed, and I couldn't see your face from such a far distance. You were moving slowly, yet far more quickly. Maybe my dreaming had a way of speeding things up, much like how movies use jump cuts to convey time gone past. I didn't know why you were out there in the fields; only that you had to be out there.

I loved the moon, but even it didn't illuminate why you hung up. It had a face much like yours, full of gray silences, startling brightnesses punctuated without warning. I wanted to call out to you, to insist that you come to my place where a fire could thaw your bones, but you'd turned your back against me. You'd turned yourself into a shadow as black as tar.

That hurt. I'd mourned for a lost love before, and I knew I didn't have the strength to mourn again. Not while you were still alive, not while you'd told me you'd passed all the necessary tests.

"Me too."

You patted my knee in your car that first night I came to your house. Looking back, I realize you must've lost a large number of friends. You were of that generation who'd heard the phrase "He's dead now" one time too many. You never told me about them, but I didn't need to ask.

Guys my age have had so little direct experience with friends dying from AIDS, and I saw the crow's feet around your eyes. You'd alluded to having been out for a long time, having visited the city many times over the years, and trying out one relationship after another, all of which lasted a few months each. Your past was gauzy, full of whispers slipping through the sealed cracks of your house. The whispers tiptoed on cat's feet made of wind chill, suggesting inchoate stories of no beginning, middle, or end. You'd loved, and they'd died, and you'd decided to try again.

So was the endless cycle, the winding road you'd chosen to take.

In the static electricity of your silences, I found myself remembering the many ways we'd made love. I know you'd react negatively to my phrase "made love," but there is no better description of how you handled me. At first we were rough and aggressive; almost angry with each other, yet we weren't. Don't you remember? You'd said that I was the best fuck of your life. You kept wiping the sweat off your brow.

You too were the best fuck of my life.

Even though you were in your fifties, I was agog at your physical perfection. Here were the perfectly rounded pecs, aswirl with fur with each nipple perking up like a cherry topping a sundae. Here was the belly, an atlas of endless pleasure when I rubbed my face across its sea of fur and when I saw your stomach muscles knot each time you thrust harder into me. Here were the tree trunks of your thighs holding you up like the redwood you were when you towered above me, gripping the branches of my sapling body. Here were the mountainous ridges of your shoulders, bristled with fur that stood firm even when I held onto them. Here was your neck, strong as a horse galloping across field, and it took all my might to hang on when you shifted speed, tempo, angle. Here was your forested beard, seasoning mine with salt and pepper as you rubbed it against me, until I felt properly roasted. Here was your tongue, long as a fishing pole darting so sharply for the trout of my tongue, hooking me, reeling me closer down your throat was the sweetest bait I'd ever known. Here was your nose, the chunk of marble that's given many a sculptor the hardest time when hacking away, and yet shiny and smooth when my nose caressed yours. But more than anything else, I saw the entire universe open up in the telescope of your galaxy eyes. You were the moon, the stars, the cosmos. I was sucked into your black hole of need, and I didn't need a theory to explain why I was here on this lonely planet.

When, then, did you decide I didn't exist in your cosmos? Were you indeed full of ego like Zeus, the Greek god who hadn't yet learned the errors of his ways? The problem with being a god is the loneliness of being at the top. The universe is full of ghosts whose names and stories we will never uncover no matter how rigorously we make scientific and technological advancements. No matter how we may delude ourselves, we will never be superheroes.

Sometimes, when I feel that intense ache for you, the kind that just about claws my heart into splinters, I pull up the pillows and wrap them in a fleece blanket so they turn into a big mass, something like your wide back that I can lean against while I sleep. I imagine the soft fleece to be the same thing as your furry back, but it's missing the rise and drop of your breathing.

I felt like a child next to you.

Now I feel orphaned.

My heart is all ashes. One puff of air, and I'm gone.

Winter nights up north fill the darkest of hours, the most urgent of needs. If I don't move for the first ten minutes inside my bed, the heavy blankets will collect the heat from my body like gold and spread it all around. I might feel a little nip in the air as I sleep, but my body will feel heavenly.

Yet with you, I've turned cold as a corpse. I have forgotten to dream.

I am a blank sheet of ice.

Shorn of the frillery of dreams, I am immaculate. No bumps or bubbles anywhere.

You can skate across me and know that I would never crack. You can crisscross and make figure eights. You could scratch scars all across my face so the rivulets of my tears from joy would line them. I am an atlas in parched hunger, a footnote in ache.

Mornings when I awake, I still feel rapturous. The air is cold, but the dreams that blanket me keep me warm as I tiptoe on the chilly floor to the bathroom for a quick piss before I turn on the hot water for my shower.

I still think of that moment when I caught you naked, your right shin dangling. The memory of tasting the most private part of you is what has kept me warm with wonder.

MOONLIGHT, CAKED OF ASH

Did you love well what you very soon left?
Come home and take me in your arms and take
away this stomach ache, headache, heartache.
—Marilyn Hacker

J AMES, make me your Saturday night cigar.

Snip one end of my paper-browned heart right here and see the dried innards of my soul rolled so neatly. Light me up with your match, and watch me burn hazily as you draw each flake of ash and flavor deep into your mouth, and breathe out my soul. Let my ashes cascade slowly like snowflakes on your shoulders on cold nights when you are in need of a man to soothe the chill of loneliness deep in your marrow.

For you I would give up my books.

For you I would give up my dead-end job.

For you I would give up my body, my heart, my soul.

Draw me into you again, and again.

Each breath of smoke rises like a coil of rope from the pit of your guts reaching down like a hungry hand into the pit of my stomach. Each puff of smoke is an umbilical cord that must never be severed.

We are a family of men and smoke.

You drift anywhere in the air everywhere.

This blood, made of ash and ether, shall not break.

I grew up on a farm just outside a small town. It's the kind of place where parents resign themselves to the reality of losing their children to elsewhere for college and jobs. The kids who stay behind are the ones who get all the love from their parents, and the kids who return for visits are always wondering if they'd done their parents wrong. The people left behind in small towns can't see beyond the periphery of their places even when they can see on television how much the world is changing. They don't want to believe such changes are happening, because to do so would mean acknowledging that they had been wrong all along. What would that make them look like? Fools?

Right.

That's why I haven't visited my own family in years.

Each time I hear a woman cough, I think of Mom.

I don't recall the times she must've kissed me, but the smell of her is woven into the tiny clouds of smoke I walk through where smokers stand outside the front doors of office buildings. Their days are numbered. Soon they will go underground and learn how to roll their own cigarettes, much like how marijuana users figured out how to grow better and more potent cannabis in the privacy of their basements.

How I long to draw again the aroma of you, feeling dizzy with desire.

I don't know if you still remember all our weekends together, but our second night was extraordinary. Fewer orgasms, yes, but we together were a well-oiled machine. You'd studied my body carefully with hands and tongue while I studied yours. Inhaling you made me realize that I had been only sleepwalking all my life.

Do you recall what we did on our second night together? You smoked a fat stogie right there in your bedroom. You said you needed to relax a bit, so I watched you snip off one end of a new cigar. I was afraid that you would reek of those cheap cigars that I hated whenever I passed by some old men sitting on the stoop in my neighborhood. You caught the expression on my face. You said, "Don't worry. It's a great piece."

Then you struck a match.

Somehow that flame lit me up. The way it flickered across your eyes as you focused on drawing that first puff. The way you softened a little after exhaling. The way you rested on the bed, with your legs wide open. "Come here," you whispered.

I crept close to you. I didn't know what you wanted. I caught a sniff of the smoke that wafted from your cigar. You were right. It didn't produce that sickly cough I'd usually experienced around cheap cigars. I was surprised.

You said, "Open your mouth."

I did. I felt strange when you took a hit from your cigar and leaned forward to my face. You sealed my lips with yours and exhaled the smoke right into my mouth. The ether felt intense, and I coughed. "Sorry." My eyes watered briefly.

"Let's try again."

"Why?"

"It turns me on, okay?"

I nodded.

When you were ready to exhale, I opened my mouth and closed my eyes. I felt your lips on mine, and a gentle puff tumbled into me. I still felt the urge to cough, but I squelched it. I felt strangely contented. The smoke had been inside you, and it was now inside me.

We exchanged puffs like that for a while. I noted the stiffness of your erection, and you moaned when I stroked you while you propelled another puff into me. I was taken aback when I felt the quiver of your cock spasming. The inhalation of your puffs didn't turn me on at all, but I was surprised by your forceful orgasm.

Please come back into my life and light up that stogie again.

I was clean-shaven for the longest time. Of course, I'd always noticed men with scruff, but they always seemed to be from a different planet. Many of them intimidated me even when they blinked crazily on my gaydar. A few of them gave me the look of want, but I was too afraid. I didn't think I was worthy of such hotness.

But when I saw a few guys my age growing facial fur, I thought to do the same. Growing my first beard was surreal and exciting at the same time. I was morphing into someone I barely knew. Yes, there in the mirror was my face and its features I'd known all my life, but who knew that the fur growing like blades of moss could change the topography of my face so dramatically?

I thought of those guys I'd seen on tractors in the summer and snowplows in the winter where I grew up. They didn't always know who I was, but they were never standoffish with me. I was a male, and that was more than enough for them to acknowledge me with a nod while on their jobs. In my adolescent fantasies I'd never thought of the possibility of having sex with any of them except for Larry Fruell. He was the closest I'd ever come to feeling the possibility of attraction, of sex. I loved how his fingertips and nails were cracked and embedded with traces of grease. His hands were thick with muscle, and his shoulders were rangy. His jeans slipped a bit below the waist because he'd never tightened his belt enough. He had the flattest ass I'd ever seen on anyone. But more than anything, it was the orange fire of his beard that drew my attention no matter where he was. He was the first bear god who'd inspired in me the notion of oral worship in the halls of my fantasies. Once I saw Larry up close in the bike shop for the first time, I forgot all about the kneeling-and-standing-by-rote rituals of Mass on Sundays. Men like Larry had become my new religion, and I worshipped them from afar all the time. I was the only disciple in the church of one, which had no name; I did not have a Bible nor did I know how to write such a holy book. I was filled with scenarios of being naked with them and touching them all over. I hadn't then known it was possible to have anal sex. After all, I was only fifteen.

I wanted to cry out hymns of ecstasy there in my bedroom, but I had to learn the songs of silence every time I lay there on my bed and offered up myself once again to the heavens where beer-bellied truckers and squat tavern drinkers and solid-chested farmers lolled around the altar where I was to pay my respects. They weren't always naked, and that was fine. I hadn't yet seen enough variety of cocks to know the amazing moods possible with flaccid folds, growing thicknesses, and leaking hardness. All I knew then was that the cocks of my classmates in the showers after swim practice intrigued me, but I'd intuited that the cocks of men who'd worked hard with their bodies had to be different. All that physical labor had to have an effect on their dicks. I'd gauged the bulges of these men. I never saw the exact outlines of their genitals, but I could deduce from the way their jeans cupped them that they had to be far bigger than those of boys my age.

My bed late at night was my hallowed altar where I'd offered up the sacrifice of my milky blood in exchange for the slightest hello from them. Didn't matter if they knew me or not. Boys my age lost my interest. Guys who weren't fastidious and studious like my schoolteachers compelled my eyes. I still read books, but I was filled with longing for that otherness, that tenderness, that rawness of energy pent up not only between my legs but also between an experienced man's legs. Wanting an older man because of his age wasn't the reason I'd wanted him; I wanted someone who wasn't a boy, who wasn't one of those arrogant football jocks. I wanted to touch skin that had a hint of wear and tear in it, and seeing the abundant hair on forearms drove me crazy. What's more, many of these men didn't give me attitude. I was probably just a slightly bookish teenager to them.

When I saw you sitting at that table at the VFW Hall, alone that night, I felt as if you were my adolescence come to life. You were the daddy bear I didn't know I was looking for until I laid my eyes on you.

Way up north where I grew up, all sorts of loners have chosen to live out in the country, so we have this *laissez-faire* attitude about folks who are a little odd. We don't bother them, and they don't bother us. At most they'd say hi to us in the checkout aisle in a hardware store, and we'd know nothing more about them beyond what they wore and what kind of truck they drove. This is the way things are up north.

My father was a slender man. The joke in my family was that we were all born like Dad, and that once we hit our thirties, we become like Mom, who was a bit heavy. I can see that happening to my own body, and that I look like her doesn't make me feel masculine. I do have her lips and eyes, but I move just like my Dad. He walks quickly and nimbly, and he isn't always patient with others. Of all his sons, I'm the most stubborn. If I make up my mind, that's pretty much it.

Dad is the same way.

I knew it was pointless to argue with him once he banished me from his house.

Mom shrugged her shoulders. She knew that it was just as pointless.

When I came up north, she would come over to my sister Sally's house. We'd talk, but it wasn't the same. Mom acted as if she was committing a crime. Sometimes I got the impression she didn't want to know me too well. I was too bookish, too smarty-arty for her. How do you explain to a woman who's never gone to college that literature isn't about being smart? Literature is reading about people's lives and caring for them as if they were your own flesh and blood. It's about appreciating the craft and the clarity that comes from telling a good story. It's about seeing yourself in the characters and discovering things you hadn't realized before. Which is exactly what we do with the people in our lives. Mom had never cared to read much. Dad never finished college either. They married right out of high school and started having babies right after. Same old story. No need to go into details.

After all, you've grown up with people like my parents.

Though Mom's been dead for twelve years, not a day goes by when I don't think about her. She is everywhere. When I see a woman walk with her child across the street from where I stand in Brewe Sisters, I think of her.

Mom had married a difficult man, and she bore him five children, four of whom didn't move too far from home and gave her grandchildren. Being the youngest, I was the only one of her kids who went off to college, and I didn't give her a grandchild. She was absolutely devoted to her grandchildren. I think they gave her a reprieve from Dad.

I never thought he could be considered abusive until years later. He never drank, but there were moments we were growing up, when he became frustrated with crops and bills and everything, that he used a hollow rubber cord to whip us. We kids had to stay in line, much like the von Trapp family in *The Sound of Music*. We never talked about it, even when we were completely alone in the house. We were afraid to whisper even in the dark. We intuited it was wrong, but who were we to argue with Dad?

To argue with him was to risk death.

My third oldest brother, Sammy, spouted off at Dad once because he didn't like the curfew. He wanted to go drinking with his buddies on his last weekend of high school. Without a word, Dad moved quickly and slammed a nice one on Sammy's chin. He fell backward against two kitchen chairs, which broke in parts. His head hit the edge of the table. He collapsed to the floor.

All of us stood still.

Mom rushed to Sammy's aid.

Dad said, "When you're feeling better, you can fix those damn chairs."

He walked out of the room.

I couldn't believe that no one had suggested he go to the hospital.

"Shouldn't he see a doctor or something?" I asked.

Mom turned and looked at me coldly. "There's no blood. See?" She looked at Sammy. "No blood. Don't need to take him there. Just some rest, and he'll be fine."

Her dismissal was breathtaking.

Sammy seemed to have recovered well, but a few years later he slipped on a patch of ice on the sidewalk downtown and hit his head on a streetlamp. They did a X-ray or a MRI on him, and it turned out that he had sustained a permanent crack from that kitchen table.

He was never quite the same again. He had a mild form of short-term memory loss, and he had the sad habit of walking into a room and standing still for a few minutes, trying to remember what he'd come into the room for. But if you put him out in the fields, he knew what to do. He was a born farmer.

I wanted to remind Dad that Sammy's condition was his fault, but I was afraid he'd hit me too.

Growing up, I came to link the smell of freshly brewed coffee with the snarl of cigarette smoke on those cold mornings when I got up early for school. When Mom wasn't busy stirring oatmeal for us, she sat by the kitchen window and looked out on the road we lived on. I saw the ache of wanderlust in her eyes, but she never said anything.

One day, when I came home with a report card columned with As, she looked quietly into my eyes. "Keep doing this, whatever you're doing, and then go."

"What are you talking about?" I was fourteen.

"You're too smart for around here. You need to go college."

"I don't want to—"

Her look of hardness silenced me. She coughed again after she took a deep drag on her cigarette. "Don't you be making my mistakes, you hear?"

College seemed a lifetime away, but she insisted that I apply for it. It was important to her that I live in a big city. That had been her biggest dream while growing up on the farm, but she had been too weak to stand up to Dad. She loved him, but she didn't know if she loved her dreams more. In that moment of weakness she married him and bore his children.

When I told her that I'd gotten into the university, she wouldn't let me go as she cried into my shoulder. She kept crying into my shoulder. "Please don't tell Dad yet." She stopped. "Not for a while yet anyway. He won't take it well."

Once I filled out the financial aid paperwork, I had to tell Dad. I needed his signature on some forms, and I needed a copy of his income tax return for proof of his income. It was after dinner. It was barely spring, but the islands of snow were receding into the ocean of grass. The first wind of balm hadn't yet arrived, but I was already feeling my chest fluffed up like a robin from so much pride, promise, excitement. Everything around me I knew I would leave after my high school graduation, and this I didn't mourn. I knew many of my classmates would go to the community college two towns over, and a few would be going to the other university further up north. I think out of my graduating class of forty-four people, only three of us were moving south to the big city. I didn't really like either one of them, but that was okay. I didn't expect to remain friends with them anyway. The idea of my new university having over twenty-five thousand students, which was six times the entire population of my hometown, boggled my mind. And that number didn't include the rest of the city itself! The city had three other smaller colleges as well.

"Dad," I said. "I need to ask you about something."

He looked up sternly from his pipe smoking. I'd rarely asked him for anything. I had been so afraid of him all my life, but I knew if there was one last thing I wanted from him, it was this: his signature. I needed to demonstrate that my parents hadn't made enough to be forced to pay for my education. I needed a raft of scholarships and probably a loan to carry me through. I knew I'd have to work very hard, but asking Dad was the hardest thing I'd ever done.

"Um, I need you to sign some forms."

"Whatever for?"

"Well, I'm going to need financial aid for college."

He turned quiet. It wasn't the kind of silence I'd expected from him. This was a soft quiet. None of that hardness about him.

"I know you don't make a lot of money, but they need to see proof. That way I can apply for loans and stuff."

He spoke in a voice so soft I wasn't sure if I'd heard him right. "So you're really going away?"

I nodded. "I thought you knew," I lied. Everyone had known, but we were all afraid he'd lash out at me for leaving him behind, for not proving my allegiance to him. I was surprised by his response.

"Well." He looked into the cup of his pipe. "Bring me the forms."

I pulled them out of the big envelope and placed them in front of him.

I'd never loved my father as much as I'd loved him in that moment. With each gnarly John Hancock of his, he was freeing me from the prison of prairie I'd grown up in. I'd felt guilty many times about reading so many library books when he insisted that I join my siblings in weeding the garden in the back and helping out in the barn. I weeded, of course, but only in the early morning when the sun wasn't so intense.

The next day I bicycled the six miles to the post office in town and sent off the forms the first thing for fear of Dad suddenly demanding that I retract them. He looked at me differently for a long time after that, and Mom smiled at me more and more behind his back.

One night, when Dad was out in the barn fixing a troublesome tractor, Mom exclaimed out of the blue in the kitchen when I was about to go upstairs to my bedroom: "So you're *really* going away!" There was so much emotion in her voice: pride, fear, love, anxiety. "Please don't forget about me." This was the week before I bought the one-way bus ticket to the city. I was to attend the New Student

Orientation the following week, and I had never been to the city. I was tremulous with excitement.

"I won't."

"Please. Don't. I'm your mother, you know."

"Yes, Mom."

"I remember what it was like when I left home to move into this house. I was so full of hopes and stuff, and . . . You kids were the best thing that ever happened to me. Please just don't be like me and look back, okay? Just *go*."

"I'm not going to forget you, Mom."

"You better not!" She broke into a laugh.

I didn't know then that she was trying to explain that in the moment of departure, one leaves behind the shell of one's old self for a thicker shell of one's new self. She didn't have the words, but knowing what I know now, I see how words had failed her. She had been a ghost all her life, and she wanted me to revive her from the dead the minute I climbed up the steps onto the bus. She would bless me with all her hopes and dreams, and anoint me with a single hand wave as I waved goodbye to her.

Of course, Dad wouldn't wave. He would stand next to her, wondering what was happening now. I believe that when he was alone in the fields, he would wonder what he'd done to drive me away, never realizing that the way his own father had raised him wasn't suitable for these modern times. Discipline cracked with the whip, which would inspire a great deal of fear in anyone's heart, wasn't the same thing as love. He'd never comprehend that just because he had fathered a child, he couldn't count on undying allegiance. The connection from his sperm wasn't enough; he had to prove himself worthy of that allegiance as well. This he'd never understood about fatherhood.

Hidden out in the prairie, he and I were on a wool blanket with bits of hay on it when we stripped down to expose ourselves to the sun, clouds, skies. Cars and trucks rumbled on the two-lane road in the distance. It was one of those afternoons when I suddenly didn't have a chore that needed to be done right away. There he was: fondling himself by the cow stalls when he was supposed to be shoveling manure away from the barn. He didn't seem surprised or feel the need to pull up his pants, as if he'd been expecting me to show up. He was a migrant worker, rather like a drifter, I suppose, but he had the most beautiful brown eyes. He looked up into mine, and I don't know how he knew my most-*secret* secret. "You play with yourself over there?" He pointed to the fallow land of shoulder-high prairie grass across the road from my house. I nodded yes. I went inside my house and retrieved a library book and my wool blanket, which still had bits of hay, across the road. Minutes later, he followed the path of broken stalks and found me pretending to read. He lay down beside me. I was electrified when he touched me through my pants. He smiled so sweetly when we stripped down to our leaking nubs. I didn't know that a man could be interested in touching another. I didn't last long under his agile ministrations, and he didn't, either. He was fired not long after, never found out why, but in those golden moments he had redeemed me with his power of touch.

Ah, the city! My city—certainly not Manhattan, the pinnacle of a teeming Gotham, overridden with people and cockroaches— stood tall no matter where I looked. It didn't matter how far away the skyscrapers were from the campus where I lived. They stood taller, with sharp corners unlike the cylindrical silos, and shimmered mirrored clouds drifting across the sky. It was also a clear reminder that I wasn't living up north, the great land of nothing but tall prairie grass if not corn and beets and potatoes. There was no *land* here, no sense of it at all, except in cultivated pockets of green that cropped up here and there throughout the city. It wasn't the same. Land to me was a place where nothing felt *too* planned; just happened to be there. No one posted a NO TRESPASSING sign or a NO SMOKING sign. The sky was free of distractions;

maybe a bird, but certainly not a horizon of tall buildings nudging the clouds away. The land of childhood was where I could push down tall grasses to make a bowl of sorts that I could lie down in and look up at the sky with my head resting on my hands. The buzz nearby didn't have the sound of people; just the tick of insects, the swoop of birds, the whoosh of wind. The earth breathed easily beneath my body. Everything else felt temporary, even when plated over with sidewalk and pavement. Many buildings in town were old, but it was doubtful they'd last another century.

This I hadn't realized when I first ventured alone off campus in my first month away from home. During the New Student Orientation, we students had learned how to take public buses and navigate the city's downtown. I was quiet the entire week, just simply absorbed the organized chaos of so many people crossing the streets, waiting in line at the checkout aisles, and filling the buses. At first I was amazed. There was no such thing as a rush hour in my hometown. Most cashiers in town knew who I was because they'd known my father, brothers, sister, and mother. I was a Badamore, and that was all they'd needed to know when they gave me a receipt with my change. But here, I was only a college student with no name. Feeling like a nobody overwhelmed me, almost frightened me into staying put on campus. I overheard snippets of conversation about who'd gone where and done what the night before; it sounded terribly exciting, but I didn't feel like becoming one of those eternally hip kids I'd disliked in high school. It was much better for me to get out there, on foot whenever possible, and discover the city on my own, and discover I did.

I didn't want to go to the famous landmarks. Too boring. I had seen pictures of them, and riding by some of them on the bus disappointed me. That was all? What was the big deal? They didn't seem all that large, or even interesting to look at. They looked better on the postcards, sad and lonely in their swivel pockets in the campus bookstore. No, no touristy landmarks for me. Instead, I went looking for neighborhoods that had no name, at least not the ones that appeared in *Fodor's*. My favorite neighborhood of all was also the city's most notorious. In Laronde, which lay west of downtown, the apartment buildings were squat; almost run down. You could almost smell the whiskey in the air when you walked by. The sidewalk gutters were clogged with cigarette butts and broken beer bottles and chicken bones. Some of the cars had a lot of duct tape holding up shattered windows. Old men clustered on stoops and carried on in loud voices with tiny bottles sheathed in flimsy paper bags. Some buildings had windows boarded up with plywood. I instinctively understood that this was not a safe area, but it felt real in a perverted way; poverty, drugs, prostitution were rampant here. I knew of some students living here and there as the rents were incredibly cheap. Some got mugged, of course, so I didn't dare come here at night. In the stark glare of day, I saw glints of flint in everyone's eyes whenever I happened to look up with a fleeting question of wonder. I asked, and they answered with their eyes. The city had been cruel to them, and I was to make sure that whatever happened to them was not to happen to me. This I understood.

The land up north still cast a long shadow over the city where I explored on weekends. I longed to see the sun set without a building in the way; felt a pang of ache when I realized it was harvest season. I was surprised. Harvesting is such brutal, interminable work involving many people for long hours. I rarely saw my father and brothers during that time, and Mom and other women always made meals that were easy to consume quickly out on the fields. They also canned pickles and other vegetables. Somehow the focus on food meant they were making the kitchen a *home*, even if temporarily as they bustled and bumped into each other with a laugh. Up north I was just a boy who loved to read, and what was I here now? Not even a Badamore.

When I went downstate for college, I looked in the local papers for anything to do with gay people. I didn't have to try hard. There was a gay bookstore called Adam and Steve's Bookstore on Speck Street. I bought a copy of *Gayellow Pages*. That guide opened my eyes to what was available in my new city and all over America. There were all sorts of interests ranging from Buddhism to photography, and all sorts of businesses that catered to the gay community. I felt I'd found a home of sorts. I felt saved. It didn't matter if I couldn't always get laid in the clubs. I was dazzled by the variety of men who mingled in the bars, and for a long while, that was enough. I was still frightened about catching AIDS, so I played very, *very* safely. I was always careful not to taste a man's cum. I didn't care if the guy assured me that he had tested negative the week before. Didn't matter. I wasn't going to end up in the hospital with an infamous disease and have Dad say, "I told you so."

Seeing that I wasn't alone for the first time was what gave me the strength to tell my parents about myself the day after Thanksgiving.

Mom said, "You need to see Father Clovis right away. Get that fixed."

"I'm fine. I don't need help."

Dad said nothing for a moment. If you want to amass a lot of emotional power with anyone, say very little, and when you finally say anything, make it unforgettable. You will earn a lot of respect that way. "Well, as long as you suck dick, you can't stay here. Get out."

Mom gasped.

I went upstairs, packed my stuff, and walked out. I didn't even look back. It would be quite a walk back to the bus station in town. Nevertheless I set off.

I was brimming full of emotions, helping me forget how far I had left to walk. I thought of everything, and I thought of nothing. I vacillated in the twilight of rage and sadness. I was grateful that it wasn't too cold for November.

I heard a car slow down beside me.

I looked up.

My heart stopped.

It was Larry Fruell, now a heavyset man in his forties. I used to have a major crush on him when I was a teenager. I had prayed that my ten-speed bike would clutch and break down more often so I could see him, but he always did too good a repair job with my bike. His long hair back then was a mix of blond and orange, and he had a scruffy beard. Pale blue eyes, though. They were so gentle whenever I looked into them.

He was the first man I'd later recognize as a bear. He was married with three kids. What mattered was that I was afraid of having sex with anyone.

"Need a lift?"

I leaned down to look at him. His hair was shorter, almost a crew cut, and he only wore a mustache that looked like frayed toothbrush bristles. His belly seemed to rub against the steering wheel. But he still looked hot. "Uh, I need to go to town."

"Sure. I'm headed thataway."

I got into the car.

"You're Billy Badamore, right?"

"Yeah."

"Well, good to see you again." He extended his hand.

I nearly melted when I felt the warmth of his thick hand, but I kept my cool.

"How come your folks aren't giving you a ride?"

"It's kinda complicated."

We rode silently for a few minutes. The land looked more desolate with its thin blankets of snow.

He turned to me. "You sure you don't wanna talk about it?"

"You can't tell anyone, okay? My parents would kill me if everyone in town knew about me."

"You're gay?"

My jaw dropped. "How did you know?"

"Come on, Billy. You were looking at me all the time."

I winced from embarrassment.

"It's okay. I'm not gonna tell. I used to have a buddy who sucked me off on a regular basis. Then he moved away, and I met Sheryl, and . . . you know."

"You're bisexual?"

He turned to me. "God, no. Just that queers suck dick better than women do." He groped himself. "Man. I could use a blow job right now."

We ended up in the back room of his bike shop. It was closed for the season, so he kept the lights turned off. It was cold, but the pent-up desire I had for him made me feel warm as I knelt before him. I had always been wary of swallowing, but I figured that if he was straight, he would be disease-free.

I choked on it as I wasn't used to doing that, and he laughed.

I felt embarrassed.

"Hey, Billy. I see you got a boner there. Take care of it."

"Are you gonna watch?"

"No. I don't get off on watching guys beat off. The toilet's over there."

I felt so dirty in that tiny bathroom with its broken mirror above the sink. The chill seeped deep into my bones, and I was too soft to shoot. If he'd allowed me to kiss him, or even hugged me, I'd have felt less dirty.

When I got out of the bathroom, he looked up from the counter. "Feel better?"

"Yes," I lied.

"The next bus leaves in twenty minutes. I checked."

"Thanks."

"Anytime. Let me know when you want to—you know, okay?"

I nodded.

On the bus ride back to the city, I felt disgusted with myself. I would never do that again. I couldn't understand the appeal of sucking straight men off without any reciprocation. Doing that would reinforce their hierarchical place in society. Once was enough.

In the mid-nineties, when I first saw the *Bear* magazine in the back racks in Adam & Steve's Bookstore, I couldn't believe the center-folds. They were furry, somewhat schlubby, and usually older with a bit of wear and tear, and I got hard, which surprised me. Some of these guys had average-sized cocks. I couldn't believe it. They were like anti-porn stars. I was in my mid-twenties, and it was the first time I'd heard of the bear community! I was so overjoyed with the discovery, but my gay friends gave me the eyes-rolling-whatever look when I tried to explain how important it was to accept your own body as it was and rebel against the twink body-fascist standards so prevalent in the bar culture.

I wanted in with those trucker-type guys who had fur on their bodies and who looked good naked in their unbuttoned flannel shirts and baseball caps. I couldn't believe that those models, who reminded me of the guys I'd seen while growing up, could be gay. They'd even listed what they were into sexually along with their pictorials, and just knowing what they were into, even if it wasn't all of what I was into at the time, was more than enough to get me stiff. But where were the local bears?

I saw in the *Gayze* newspaper a small ad announcing the third annual OctoBear Dance at the VFW Hall. I couldn't wait. For the occasion, I decided to wear a flannel shirt and jeans. I spent twenty minutes trying to decide how many buttons I should leave open at the top of my chest. I didn't have a lot of chest fur, but I wanted to show that I did have some. I kept looking this way and that in the mirror when I buttoned one more, then unbuttoned two more. I wanted my friends to tag along, but none of them looked bearish. I was still a bit skinny, but I figured that as long as I didn't hold in my flabby stomach, I'd pass. I knew I'd look ridiculous in my black sneakers, but I didn't have the money for boots. I'd just graduated with a MFA the year before, so I was working full-time at Brewe Sisters, and I'd moved in with my lesbian housemates six months before.

I walked the mile and half from my house to the hall. The orange leaves, as if lit on fire by the streetlights, fell around me as I walked closer. Everything was starting to feel like magic. And, frankly, I was horny. I had become more attuned to stocky guys on the streets and elsewhere now that I knew they had a name of their own. "Bear." I couldn't stop trailing my eyes after men in uniform, like bus drivers and cops. I didn't know if I could hold a conversation with these guys, but if we couldn't talk about anything, our bodies could speak perfectly in the same language.

I remember this one bus driver. He was a bit wide in the hips, but he had the most angular jaw I'd ever seen. There was a star cleft in his chin. He was shaven bald with his thick mustache immaculately trimmed. His eyes were flint-gray when he took in all of me in the widescreen mirror above him as he drove. He gave me a slight smile, but that was more than enough to keep me looking at him. I craned to see if he had fur on the back of his hands, always a good indicator of just how hairy he could be under all those clothes. I listened to his quiet voice when he spoke to a customer swiping her fare card. I thought of him standing before me and unzipping himself in front of everyone to reveal a huge erection. I was thinking all these thoughts while I was sipping in the sight of that bus driver. If I had been in lust with someone before, this was different. This was a far more intense lust, mainly because I now understood there were indeed others who appreciated my kind of men, and these guys had to know how they could be appreciated so easily.

I prayed that the bus driver would be at the dance.

I prayed that the janitor from the building where I worked would be there.

I prayed that all the construction workers I'd lusted after would all be there.

It was ten minutes past eight when I showed up. The dance ran from seven to eleven p.m., but I didn't want to seem too early.

At first I felt intimidated by the beefy and brawny men standing around with their beers. They were in their lumberjack drag, and they were hot. Seeing so many men with *beards* all in one place was almost too much. I wanted to go into the men's restroom and beat off. I was that horny.

I must've looked forlorn with my beer in a plastic cup. I've never liked the taste of beer, but I wanted that badly to fit in with them. I wanted to be one of those guys who had beefy friends. I stood by the doors, debating whether I should bolt or not. The music was all disco, and all before my time. A lot of shirtless guys danced their bellies off. Some of them had really flabby pecs, and I was afraid that those obese guys would find me attractive. I tried to look cool—whatever that meant—whenever guys glanced my way, but because I was alone, I looked worse than uncool. I was never going to fit in there. I wanted to melt into the cement-blocked wall behind me.

Then a short balding potbellied man strode up to me. I didn't know that the bear community was developing their own jargon, but today everyone would've called him a "pocket bear." He looked cute in his own way, but he didn't do the lumberjack stuff. He wore a striped shirt and jeans and Reeboks; a complete dork. Still, I was happy that someone said hello to me. Even if he was only five feet tall.

"Hi, I'm Craig Gorman." He extended his hand.

"Bill Badamore."

Craig and I stood by the wall. I listened while he did all the talking. All I had to do was to ask a question, and off he went. I didn't know it then, but he had been extremely nervous about approaching me. He was a computer programmer, and he was quite excited that the Internet, which I hadn't known much about then, was becoming more and more accessible to the masses. He was working for the company that ran CompuServe. He babbled about forthcoming changes in the tech specs for telephone modems. I thought "modem" was a very odd word at the time.

He took my hand and stroked my palm with his thumb while he looked up into my eyes. "I like you." Did you know how much that meant to me, James? So many people are so afraid of being direct with their feelings.

"Thank you." I squeezed his hand back.

He lit up.

Of course I had to go home with him that night.

In his condo a few blocks away, we were all over each other. He wasn't as furry as I'd hoped, but I didn't care. I was making love to a *bear*. Soon, I thought, I'd be one of them. He'd introduce me to his furry friends, and among them I'd meet my future husbear.

I ended up falling for Craig instead.

All my life I slept in percale sheets until I met Craig. They scratched against my elbows when I turned over, so I wore long-sleeved pajama tops. I didn't know that there could be softer sheets that my bare skin could luxuriate in. I'd always bought the cheapest sheets available.

When I stayed overnight at Craig's place for the first time, I couldn't get over how gentle a bed sheet could be. Craig kept laughing at how I rubbed my body against so much flannel. I just couldn't get over how *loved* I felt in that bed. Of course, Craig and I had wonderful sex, but the 400-thread count flannel surrounding my body felt like a blanket of arms wrapped around me. The flannel did not want to let me go, and I did not want to wake up. The wintry dreams I had were full of snowflakes and stars, and I scarcely noticed it when Craig snuggled up to me.

The very next day I charged a new set of flannel sheets at Jaxson's downtown. I didn't care that they were so expensive, but I simply had to have flannel on my bed. I felt horror at the idea of having to wash them first, but I followed the instructions on the label. It was such a joy to pull the still-warm sheets over the corners of my bed, and right there, on my bed, were bright red sheets, precombed to prevent excessive pilling. I went to bed early and thought of Craig, and I fell asleep just like that.

Later, when Craig died, I took all of his flannel sets except for the one still on his bed. I slept in those sheets for years until each set, one by one, turned thin in spots and ripped holes in the corner seams. My heart was feeling the same way when I first saw you.

I needed a new set of sheets, a new winter, a new beginning.

When I slept in your flannel-covered bed the first night, I felt right at home. I thought that you were perhaps the one to make the breath of Craig fade from my pillows. He was a wisp, and you were a redwood full of sunlight and shade. I wanted you to loom above all that I'd known. You were the Adam, strong and majestic enough to inspire love in the stoniest of hearts deep inside men, and you'd lead me into the great Garden of Eden where there was enough warmth from the sun to keep us fully naked without a shiver. I would walk with you, unashamed of my own body, and hold your hand while we walked among the trees and ate one fruit after another. Our cries of pleasure from making love would echo across the land. Your virility would awaken desire in the eyes of others equally naked, and I would be proud to join others in those sudden fits of passion. Your kisses would redeem me from all those years of living death.

I was a dead man who passed as alive when I met you. The magic of you was pure oxygen coming straight down from Mount Everest. Suddenly I could breathe the crispness of hope all over again. For the first time in years, I didn't think about Craig or the fear of contracting *it*. You made me feel like anything was possible, especially with the orgasms we shared. You were fire in flannel.

Craig and I never got around to living together. He wanted me to move in with him, but I was still in my mid-twenties. Each time I went out to bear events with him and met all his gorgeous friends, I felt more and more afraid to live with him. What if I cheated on him? I also didn't understand how open relationships could work.

Then he tested positive.

I was shocked, hurt, angry, fearful—the whole enchilada.

Then I became frightened. In those days it took a week to get the test results. I didn't know whether to cry or bolt each time I saw Craig. I couldn't sleep at all. It was the worst week of my life.

When I called the clinic for the results, she said, "Oh, you're negative."

Those were the three sweetest words I'd ever heard all my life.

I felt saved, redeemed, blessed.

But watching your first boyfriend wither away into bones in the nightmarish days before protease inhibitors came along was the worst way to grow up. I wasn't in my twenties anymore. I was an old man. He kept saying how much he loved me, how I should leave him, how he'd understand if I left him then. He didn't want me to remember him as a skeleton, but I couldn't abandon him. I hated hospitals, but I had to be there.

When he died, I sensed it instantly. I was sleeping alone in my bed even though I had keys to his condo. I didn't like the feeling of dread that permeated his place when he wasn't around, so I preferred to sleep in my bed. At least I didn't have to see reminders of his impending death—the insurance paperwork, the orange silos of pills, the constant piles of sheets that needed to be changed and washed. Death was the mysterious odor impossible to remove even with the toughest chemicals.

The second he died in the dark of night, I jolted awake. I hadn't known why. Two minutes later my phone rang.

"He died, right?"

"How did you know?"

"I felt him a minute ago."

James, I hate to say this, but I was so relieved when Craig died. I didn't want him to go, but he was in so much pain and agony. He didn't look himself at all. He looked like a skinny animal with buck teeth and kooky glasses. He'd become quite blind due to CMV.

Anybody who can stand by their man as he dies is good husband material. I thought that's what you were looking for. A man who'd never let you down: that's the kind of fellow I am.

The bed I slept in had turned into a flannel-lined coffin. It had only one pillow, and no room for you, Craig. You had been cremated and packed into a Mason jar. At first I didn't want to look at it or leave it out in my room because its salt-and-pepper powder in no way resembled you. It was hard to reconcile my memory of your flesh and blood with the clinical dryness of ash sealed inside a see-through jar. I hid it far back on one of the shelves in my closet and kept the door closed. It felt creepy to think that remnants of your being could be locked up in that tiny closet, but it was the only way I could sleep. There, I lay in my coffin as I floated away. Everywhere was the smoke of factory where the masked men and women, wearing white lab coats, directed single files of men and women, pockmarked with Kaposi's sarcoma and sagged with fleshy skin, one after another, into the black mouth. I knew where they were going, and the air was full of their deaths, rising and casting a white pallor across everything even on the sunniest of days.

Craig, I thought of you joining these men and women, whose faces and names have been long forgotten, in that ceaseless puff toward sky. You couldn't be contained inside the funeral home's assembly line where your body was incinerated and your sizzling ashes brushed each way and then into that jar. You couldn't have been reduced to a few mere pounds. Not possible. But there you were, in my hands. The jar didn't have a face or a body, but I wanted to cradle it like the child you last were in my arms before you died. I wanted to put you in a swath of sun-warmed blankets and have you fall asleep on my shoulder as I stood in the sun and swayed slowly to let you dream to the music of my body reaching out to you, singing and aching. But the weight of you was the heaviest I'd ever carried. My shoulders got sore from the yoke of your memory.

In the darkness you slept, the beautiful innocent baby that you were, and I slept too, or tried to, the awful daddy I was not to have cherished your sweetness more when you were alive in my arms.

One night I tried to inhale marijuana for the first time. A friend of my housemates, Chloë and Veena, had brought a joint over because she thought it'd help soothe my jagged nerves. Everyone knew what a walking ghost I'd become in your wake. Craig, I tried my best to look cool, hip, whatever, but I just couldn't. I coughed, sputtered. I tried to slow down my breathing, tried again. This time the smoke floated into my head, rising and roasting my brain as it spun. I didn't know what I was feeling; was I keeling over? But I felt hands on my arms; I think I was guided back to the sofa, made to sit there. I don't know what I said. All I know was that I'd felt quite light. Suddenly I thought the death of you was a big cosmic joke. I giggled at anything, riffed on the romantic things you'd done for me, went into great detail what you'd done, how foolish you were to do them for me . . . I think I dozed off. I don't remember. I felt lethargic when I woke up an hour or so later. I was confused. I thought I'd died. I was so disappointed when I realized I hadn't. The lesbians were playing cards in the dining room. I groaned when I tried to get up from the sofa. My head felt so heavy, almost like lead but worse than that when I realized how badly my head hurt, throbbed. I mumbled words like "fuckin' headache" and "aspirin" and "water." I don't think I was quite coherent then, but somehow someone gave me an aspirin and some water. When I woke again, half an hour had passed. I was so hungry, I wanted so much to pepper the salt of you over everything I ate. I needed to eat more, fill out my chest, my belly, my ass so I'd never shrink into the skeleton you were when you'd died. I would be a bundle of fat so blubbery that I couldn't sink no matter how much I wanted to drown.

Craig, the weight of you was the weight of my heart.

Of course, I didn't gain that much weight and eventually lost most of it. I didn't do pot again. The headaches and the munchies just weren't worth it, but the looks that I got from my housemates bothered me a little. It was as if I'd said things, sacrilegious things really, about Craig; that I'd become truly evil deep down inside, mocking Death in its face with my laughter. I'd kicked the loving memory of you into the dustbin of my history, and banged its lid shut loudly in case no one knew that you, my little lamb, my little love, had died. A few years would pass until my housemates told me what I'd said about you. I was so shocked, mortified; I desecrated your memory with my angry pissings. I'd pulled down my pants and squatted, figuratively speaking, of course, in front of your tombstone, and I did so with a mad glee they'd never seen in me before. In that moment, they'd thought of asking me to move out, but I'm glad they didn't.

They are the truest family in my life, and I can't bear the idea of never having them in my life. But my own family? They might as well be smoke from a factory.

In those bleak months after Craig died, I thought I would go crazy. I was seeing him everywhere. Didn't matter what the guy looked like as long as he was short. Sometimes I wanted to call out to the guy across the street and shout his name, but he'd turn to look at something else. Then it wasn't Craig anymore.

He had spoiled me. No one in my family paid me much attention, so I felt quite overwhelmed by his affections and constant fretting over me. I didn't think I was worthy of such attention. He was the one who told me, "What your family taught you was stupid. They told you weren't worthy of love. Well, I'm here now, and I'm telling you that I love you with all my stupid heart."

"You're not stupid," I said.

"What part don't you get?"

"What?"

"You don't get that I love you very much?"

"Oh, that I do."

"Then kiss me and say thank you, dammit." He looked slightly hurt, but he seemed better when I took his hand and didn't let go when we walked down Speck Street. I felt scared at first to be holding a man's hand in public, but we were in a gay neighborhood. I still felt apprehensive.

I had never seen him look so happy. It was as if he'd won a major award, and no one knew why. People walking past us didn't seem fazed by our PDA. I was relieved.

But when he got sick, I felt scared. I withdrew my hand from his, but I saw in his eyes how much he understood. I felt bad. Still do. If I'd known back then what we know now about the disease, I'd have held his hand and never let go anywhere we went. Wouldn't matter if he was frail-looking or not with his walker. But stupid me, I didn't give him what he wanted the most of all—my pride in being his man.

After Dad banished me, I didn't go back until I graduated from college four years later, and only when the foliage was in autumnal riot. I stayed with my sister, Sally. Of all my siblings, she was the most understanding, and even then, she didn't want to know the particulars of my love life. She didn't want to know anything more about Craig once I mentioned his name. The fact that he was a man was upsetting enough. I never stayed long at Sally's house. Her kids were loud and noisy, and their Pomeranian yapped nonstop at sounds that we couldn't hear from the outside. It was not a restful place.

Mom never told me much about Dad. "The same," she said.

Until Sally told me about her lung cancer, I'd never thought much about Mom's smoking. She'd always smoked. I was used to hearing her hacking coughs in the morning before she lit her first cigarette of the day. I had gotten used to the whiff of smoke in my clothes, but when I went away to college, so few people smoked that I got used to not having the stink in my clothes. When the city passed an anti-smoking ordinance for bars and restaurants,

I started feeling more alert. I hadn't realized how much second-hand smoke had affected me. I had felt slightly dragged down, but I thought that was because of the loud music and the strobe lights. Suddenly I could see everything clearly.

I went up to see Mom at the hospital every other weekend, and then three people at work quit at the same time to protest the way my asshole boss was treating them. That was how I'd become assistant manager, and that meant I couldn't go up and see Mom as often as I liked. Sally was the one who kept Dad away from the hospital when I showed up. He soon drifted further and further in the distance until I had only a few crunchy leaves of color in my hands. The tree had shorn itself of me.

The waft of freshly brewed coffee that I served my customers wasn't enough to keep my listlessness at bay. Craig had been dead for a few weeks.

Those nights I felt his ghost drift through my room and evaporate. I was angry with him for keeping me awake for so long.

I discovered that the only way I could sleep was to forget all about him.

Must I do the same with you? I don't want to.

James, you're still alive.

I don't want you to die in my dreams.

You can still come back.

I don't want you to float slowly through the smoky halls of my brain, pausing to look back now and then. I couldn't bear to see the desire aflame in your eyes again, not unless you were sure you wanted me back permanently.

With you, I felt as if I was opening up like a wheat field, an ocean rushing in, when you entered me for the first time. I wasn't tense or afraid. I couldn't stop touching the sweat sopping your chest when you grunted away. I knew I didn't exist, not in that moment when it was all about the thrusting, but I was *alive*. I felt redeemed.

Strange that I needed a tall and handsome stranger to show me a way out of that exhibition hall of ghosts. I'd thought all the doors to the land of the living were locked. I could see through the panes of glass the grass turning bright green and the buds blooming in a confetti of color. Inside, I couldn't focus my eyes on anything long enough to render sharpness in my own vision. The dust of ash covered everything. If I inhaled, I choked on the acridity of death. My feet were heavy with the weight of the dead. I couldn't move quickly enough. I had to be patient with myself. Some nights I felt as if I'd moved only one inch, but even that felt like a victory. I was a snail. I was afraid of letting light into the shell of my heart. If my first boyfriend could die within a year of meeting me, all the men would surely die after having sex with me. I was infected with fear and paranoia.

That's why I knew it was quite all right to have you as my man. Didn't matter that you had one foot. It meant that you were free of death, of illusions. It's strange how I don't remember specifically how you walked beside me. I must've floated with you because that's how you'd made me feel.

That winter walk, the only one we'd undertaken after the snow came and stayed, is a chunk of dry ice left permanently in the freezer of my heart. I'd joked that we should try something different that December afternoon.

"Like what?"

"I don't know," I said. "Hey, I know. A walk. We could take a walk out in the woods."

You glanced out the back window. The sun was half-covered by clouds. It was ten degrees, but there was only a slight wind.

"Sure."

You should've seen me stop myself from falling off the ottoman in your living room.

You walked to your bedroom and returned with a different prosthetic foot. "This is better for walking on uneven ground," you explained.

I watched you take off your jeans and swap your prosthetic feet. It may sound strange for you to hear this, but I felt honored that you didn't hide from me for the first time. I felt as if you knew I wouldn't bolt from seeing you do such a thing.

I watched you button up your sexy red Union Jack as I put on my long underwear and tucked my jeans into my Sorel boots, a carryover from the days when I lived further up north. It took us fifteen minutes to get ready with sweaters, scarves, and mittens.

God, we couldn't stop smiling at each other. Don't you remember that?

The snow was a foot, a foot and a half, deep. It had fallen earlier that morning.

The whitescape was beautiful.

An occasional trail of bird prints crisscrossed each other, and rabbit pellets had rolled like marbles down the smooth inclines.

We didn't say much.

I watched you perch your crutches forward, lift your foot, and bring up the crutches. You went ahead of me. I was in awe of the huge size of your footprints.

The clouds took to hiding the sun. It was as if the sun was cold too.

Up the hill you were like a shadow climbing further away from me, and you suddenly stopped. You leaned against a thick birch tree. You smiled at me as I grunted my way up toward you. I remembered that you used to be an avid hiker.

I was surprised when you pulled me into your arms, and I felt the hot cock of your tongue probe deep into the hole of my mouth. The tiny icicles of your beard bristles melted on my chapped lips. I couldn't stop sipping the pearl drops of you. I slaked the sweetest thirst.

I held you for the longest time.

I wanted to cry from so much happiness, but I was afraid that my tears would freeze and zip my eyelids shut.

You kissed me again. And again.

I was so surprised. You rarely showed me affection outside sex.

The land beyond the birches was level so it was easy to walk. There wasn't as much snow either. I heard birds flutter in the branches above us as they bounced from tree to tree. Maybe they were hoping we had seeds and crumbs for them.

The trees began to cluster closer and closer together until it was harder to navigate. I wanted to ask you where you were going. Was there a cabin hidden somewhere in the woods? I had hoped so. My mind's eye danced with us cuddling fiercely against the dying fire inside the dank cabin. You would tell me how much you needed me, how much you wanted me, how much you loved me.

Instead you took me inside a small clearing. "Sometimes in the summer I come here, take off my clothes, and jack off while I smoke my cigar."

You smiled at me as you held my hand, your glove in my mitten.

What happened that made you feel so cold toward me?

Sometimes when I'm lonesome, I like to remember climbing up on a haystack to look across the fields. The golden sun lathered honey all over my face. I felt all right with the world. I didn't need a book at that moment to feel alive. All I had to do was close my eyes and feel the sun caressing my face. That's why I understood your preference to stay away from the city and stick to the country.

When I wandered through the so-called "back forty" on your property, I felt as if I had entered a new world. It was calling back to the child I once was. How could I have abandoned him so? There was in you something like the father I'd longed to have in my childhood, and the eloquent silences you spoke made the child in me hum, more so when I saw how easily you wove among the birches and the cottonwoods that crowded your land. I wanted to have you embrace me in your solid arms so I could feel small again, like the boy I'd forgotten to say goodbye to in the middle of that mad rush to grow up and move away. That boy hadn't known how loved he had been, and I'd neglected to tell him so.

When you caressed my face in the darkness that first night, I felt as if I'd been touched by the hands of the sun.

Mom went through a full round of chemotherapy only once; it was too much for her. It was enough to convince her to die. She didn't want to fight anymore. Each round, lasting a few hours a week, was enough to zap her strength. She wasn't anymore a woman of enough strength and stamina to keep the house clean, look after the chickens and the garden, and pay the bills. She wanted to go to sleep and never wake up. She hated feeling weak, unable to move when there were many things that needed taking care of. Sally told me how she had to vomit into the bucket next to her bed.

I never learned how Dad dealt with it, but I imagine that to him, it was just another crisis, like how a cow might be finicky with her newborn calf and didn't want to be milked. Was she just another farm animal to him? I couldn't help but wonder. Dad had grown up on a farm without the latest equipment, so he was used to doing things the tougher way. None of that fancy stuff was necessary if he could save money. All of us siblings worked the land with him, and my three brothers became farmers. Sally married a truck driver, so she didn't see him much either. I think Dad had prepared us to expect a lot of silence from the ones we'd love. Anyone talking a bit was indeed too much for us.

I taught Composition 101 in exchange for my graduate school tuition. It was frightening at first to stand in front of fifty students at a time and explain the ins and outs of grammar and punctuation. Even though they were only a few years younger than I was, I felt old. Learning how to write essays, even if only two pages long, seemed too difficult for them.

They slothed back in their chairs.

They slurped sodas in their containers. Sometimes they were quite loud.

A few of them drifted off to sleep.

The smell of coffee was strong at the beginning of class, and evaporated by the time class ended.

For the first time I felt pity and compassion for my teachers. I had no idea how hard it was to make a lifeless subject interesting enough to keep anyone awake. But I figured that if I'd paid attention to what was hot in their world of music and movies, which was easy to do as I consider myself a pop culture aficionado to begin with, and peppered my talks with references to them, they might sit up and take notice.

One by one they did.

Not all, of course, but their sense of entitlement was occasionally breathtaking. Had they been that coddled in high school?

Their assignments broke my heart. They seemed so illiterate. How was it possible for them to have graduated from high school, let alone get into the university? I was stunned. I had always thought I was an average writer, or at least a writer with some promise, but grading their homework made me realize how much better I was as a writer.

I sought out published essays that were beautifully written and distributed photocopies.

I told them they had to copy each word in longhand. Yes, in longhand. They had to learn, to *look* at each word. I prayed that they too would take the time to think about what they were copying so it wouldn't be entirely by rote.

No one liked me that first month.

I didn't eat or sleep well. I couldn't always concentrate on my own studies. I forced myself to crank out little stories for workshopping in class. I didn't like any of them, but my classmates oohed and ahhed over them. I was stupefied. They couldn't be reading the same stuff I had written, could they?

No.

They had to be on some drug; no way anyone could rave on and on about how perfectly executed my sentences were.

"You're very sharp. You don't mince words when you write."

"You're just like Hemingway."

"I don't know about you guys, but I know I'm not going to see those haystacks the same way again."

Oh, please.

Even though I used familiar locations from my childhood, I never wrote autobiographical fiction. I was afraid of coming off as mawkish, sentimental, annoying, self-serving. No. It was much better to observe everything as if through a pair of binoculars and write down what I saw. Since I was so far away, I wouldn't be able to hear their voices so I had to imagine the stories unfolding through their actions. I felt like God overseeing his serfs, who were bad actors trying to pull off another decent show. They played characters who lived and died, and who were full of elegiac bullshit. I knew my work was bullshit, but I cranked it out anyway. I was already doubting whether I was cut out to be a writer.

It was heartbreaking when no one in Comp 101 seemed to care much about the craft of writing, let alone try to write more simply and clearly. Some of my students did work hard on writing their essays, but it was hard to grade them all. I knew I didn't have the heart to be a teacher even though that's what many Creative Writing graduates did once they got their degrees.

Each class session forced me to become someone else I hated.

After being held at arm's length within my own family, I've always wanted to be loved. It hurts a lot more than it should when strangers who barely know you beyond your name don't want to hang around and say hello. Yes, I was their teacher, and yes, they had other classes to attend, but I had become that tough asshole who was way too nitpicky about shit that nobody was ever gonna care about.

Each week, when I graded, I sought out the smallest signs of improvement, of comprehension in their homework. They did appear, but I had to hunt for them. When I found them, it felt like a little victory, and when I read other writers for the classes I was taking, I nearly cried at their mastery of language. It was such an exuberance to drink in such clarity. Semi-colons and colons were used correctly, and the Oxford comma was used consistently. Sentences were carefully strung together to achieve a certain effect. Paragraphs had stanzas of rhythm, and each page was like a pop song captured perfectly in the mind's ear. They were fearless with expressing themselves in quietly startling ways. Such music was manna from the heavens. I could listen to it nonstop.

Did I ever talk about any of this with you? No.

See, I knew that you weren't a reader; you'd told me so.

I'd never seen you as less equal to me because you didn't care for books. Oh, no. Growing up on the farm has taught me the value of common sense that a lot of book-smart people don't always have. I know what it's like to work the land. There's no romance in mind-numbing repetition.

When I spent weekends with you up north, I felt a reconnection to my past and to the family I'd lost a long time ago when I escaped to the mountain of books for safety. You didn't pass judgment on me. You gave me hope, however fleeting, that my own family would welcome me back with open arms.

Earlier today I thought of Craig. It was the seventeenth anniversary of his death. Had it been that long? Have I gotten that old?

I stood in front of the bathroom mirror at work. I saw something I hadn't quite noticed before. I leaned closer. There were a few gray hairs in my beard. Fuck. I wasn't expecting that!

I knew that day would eventually come, but I never thought it would come so soon. Time has a sneaky way of doing that to you.

All that day, when I wasn't busy serving cappuccinos and chai lattes, I prayed that my beard would turn a crisp salt-and-pepper color like yours. Now that I'd met you, I've developed a major weakness for such beards.

With each accidental glance in the mirror behind the counter, I tried to imagine how I would look at fifty, fifty-five, sixty. I couldn't imagine myself that far into the future.

Would I be still aching for the unattainable you?
Would I be happily married to someone else?
Would I be still alive?
I never thought I'd survive this long after Craig.

At his memorial service, I wasn't strong enough to read the poem I had written to remember him by. My friend Ted took the poem out of my hand, and I kept my face to the floor as I heard him try to read it with an even voice. He had met Craig a few times, but they didn't know each other well.

To Ted, he was just the boyfriend of his college friend.

Ted salvaged me. I'd lost my voice, but when he finished, a sudden beam of sunlight broke through the clouds and filtered through the stained glass window of St. Sebastian's.

Everyone looked up with surprise.

It was a sign from the heavens. It had to be.

Afterward everyone agreed that Craig had just said goodbye to everyone.

It was not the kind of goodbye I wanted.

I wanted him to say goodbye to me when we were too old to move around much. I wanted to feel his gnarly liver-spotted hand wrap around mine and hear his age-gruffed voice before I faded into my eternal slumber.

When Craig died, Mr. Death shadowed me everywhere. I didn't know what he looked like, but I knew he was there. He was transparent as air, and I didn't like that at all. I need to see something first before I can sense how I can control it. But no, he breathed down my neck each time I gazed too long at a man. Would that man give me the same kiss that Mr. Death had longed to give? I showed up at bear events because at least the men weren't skinny. They didn't have AIDS, or at least they looked like they didn't. They made me forget for a short while that Mr. Death hid like a hangnail lost inside a shadow. They wouldn't lose massive amounts of weight so quickly that they'd fade away like the legs of the Wicked Witch of the West under Dorothy Gale's house. Their weight meant they were vibrantly alive. They had been inoculated against Mr. Death's contagious kisses.

Mr. Loneliness shielded me from Mr. Death.

He and I had committed to stay together until one of us cheated with Mr. Death.

Mr. Loneliness whispered many things in my ear.

Things like: "You don't need to find anyone special because you already have me."

"Craig wouldn't want you to die. You can count on me to keep you alive."

"You don't want to die young and hurt your mother, do you?"

When I saw Mom after Craig's death, she said, "What happened to you?"

I tried to explain, but my voice was a croak. "He died."

"Who?"

"Craig."

She didn't ask any more questions. His name was enough.

Each time I went to see Mom, she floated further away. Her coughing echoed between us. Soon she had wires attached to her body, and she pounded the hospital bed with her fists. She was so angry. She had to have *one more* cigarette, dammit. She still smoked. She'd figured that as long as she was going to die, she might as well enjoy another cigarette. I didn't know what to say to her on these last few visits.

She was too busy coughing up pellets of blood.

I tried to fill the air with idle conversation about my job.

She was too busy trying not to crave another smoke.

I waved the air and tried to tell her that I loved her very much and that I would miss her when she was gone.

She stopped and stared at me. "Don't tell me that crap. I don't wanna hear that."

"Does that mean you don't want to see me again?"

"You always say the same old things. You're so full of yourself, that's what you are."

"So are you."

She looked mortified at me.

"You don't love me. That's what this has come down to. Your fucking cigarettes. You don't love me. Go ahead and die."

I stormed out of the room.

Sally gave me a major chewing-out over that, but I didn't care. She didn't seem to appreciate the fact that I was spending what little money I had left on the bus fares for up north.

It was the last time I saw Mom.

Mom, I saw you standing and wavering in the great forest of white birches, except that when I came closer, the trees weren't what they were. They were the white poles of huge cigarettes staked into the cemetery grounds. They splintered the stone and marble tombstones into flaky crumbles, and out of the smooth trunks came the spidery skeleton branches flapping in the wind, trying not to lose the tantalizing leaves of tobacco already turning red, orange, yellow, brown, the very colors of fire. Yet each time I tried to enter the forest, I found myself hitting an invisible wall. You were inside a box of no oxygen. It was the only way you could survive without nicotine. I longed to shatter that wall and have you smoke my lungs inside out so you could breathe again, and easily too.

When my phone rang in the middle of the night two months later, I was pissed. It had taken me such a long while to fall asleep this easily, and then this damn phone call. It was Dad. I was quite surprised. He never called me for anything; it had been years since I'd heard his voice.

"Oh, hi. What's up?"

"Mom died."

"What?"

"She died. Thought you should know."

"Oh, wow. Um, um . . . wow. Um, when's the funeral?"

"Three days from now."

"Okay. I'll be there."

Fuck.

I couldn't sleep the rest of that night. I felt sad that I hadn't felt her presence when she died. It was so different from when Craig died.

When Dad picked me up at the bus station, I couldn't read his wizened face. It had been so long since I'd seen him last. He didn't say much.

I didn't either. I was afraid of scaring him away, much like years later when I would be afraid of doing the same thing to you. When he dropped me off at Sally's, I knew that he'd still thought of me as unclean, that dicksucking orphan. He was too set in his ways. How can anyone convince someone so stubborn as him, or as you? Would I need to strike a match under the candle of you so that you'd jump from the intense heat of my scrutiny and melt like wax into my arms?

You are the flame, and I am only beeswax.

My brothers and I are men, but we are masters of awkwardness when we meet rather by accident. We'd never admit this to each other's faces, but if we had a say in choosing our brothers, we would never have picked each other. They are men of the land. They are well-versed in the encyclopedia of soil, water, and sun. They know how to fix gardening equipment and tractors and trucks. They inhale the poetry of the weather even when its count-the-syllables-on-the-fingers verse turns bad. With each day in the fields, they write books that will never be edited and published and read. Each moment is a sheet crumpled up and tossed in the wastebasket of nature, never to be seen again and lost to the worms of forgetfulness. They sit with their laconic observations that sound as if translated from a foreign language I thought I'd understood while growing up only to find that I've forgotten how to speak it. The land still runs deep in my bones, but the words are the true chlorophyll of my soul. With the sun of truth illuminating each row of seeds I sow, I find the crops of words easy to harvest. Survive easily on such ample feasts I do.

These men are masters of their own little domains, and I have yet to master my own. They know this, and they keep their distance from me. They know I haven't come anywhere near the amount of hard labor they've put into their own lands, for where are the crops I've yet to harvest from my years of so-called laziness with seeding so many words in the soil of my brain? Writers aren't meant to be gardeners, and yet they are asked to justify themselves over and over again with more than words. Words aren't tangible, but food on the table is. But these men forget that if it weren't for writers, they would not have movies to entertain them in the evenings after a long day of toil and soil. To tell a story well takes talent, and because they are men of the land, they find such storytellers easy to dismiss. After all, writers are supposed to be the ones with megabucks, therefore derided. Books are even worse crimes, filled with language of nothing to do with the earth and yet so much to do with the lives of others. I want to tell them otherwise, but how could I if I didn't have a man like you in my life? They'd see that not all gay people are like me, or like drag queens on television, or muscular men in full leather regalia on motorcycles in pride marches televised so heterosexuals could gawk at us as if we were zoo animals put on display for their pleasure. My brothers would've sat quietly in your presence, right there on the veranda looking out on the lonely road in the distance, for they'd realize how wrong they had been about me. I think Dad would've liked you very much. He would've been shocked to learn that you were gay. But then again if you were very masculine, he'd have felt threatened. Only straight men were allowed to be masculine, because if they weren't, how would anyone know who was queer? That wouldn't faze you at all. You would light up a cigar, and you'd be one of them in ways I could never be. I don't have a face that could hide so much feeling like yours does. I'm not a stoic man. I'm not one of those gruff guys who've seen it all and speak in laconic sentences while they drink beer and watch the news on the TV in a rundown tavern. I'm not macho enough.

In Miranden's Funeral Home, Mom lay perfectly composed with her arms crossed on her bosom. She looked a bit thinner than before, but I couldn't look at her embalmed face for long. Too freaky. It didn't look like her at all. It was as if the embalmers had found a mannequin, propped it inside the casket, made it up to look like a photograph of her, and called it a day.

I knelt before her. I didn't know what to say, what to think, what to pray. It had been a long time since I was inside a church. I'd stopped believing in the lies the Catholic Church had tried to feed me while growing up. I closed my eyes and mentally counted to fifty before I decided I was done with praying.

I went through the motions afterwards. I saw faces from my past file past me, and they seemed impressed that I was living in the city. They didn't know that city living wasn't all that it was cracked up to be. I didn't own a house, and I didn't have a car. Everyone up north owned their houses and trucks, and they didn't always have jobs.

As I nodded the whole time, I kept thinking of how I'd knelt before Mom's body; what do you say to a dead mother if you were already a ghost among her children?

The house where I grew up is a stranger.

There'd been a time when I knew its name and its moods very well: the four-bedroom house called home. Mom and Dad slept in one; two bedrooms were given to us boys, and the fourth one went to Sally. It sat centrally between the garage, barn, pasture, and the farmed fields a bit beyond. On the other side of the road was prairie land that had been left fallow for a number of years. Mrs. Marshall, the woman who owned the property across the road, didn't want anyone to touch it after her farmer husband died. I loved the wide open feel of that prairie land. Just grasses growing tall and reedy. I loved slipping away with a library book and a blanket across the road and furrowing among the grasses. Some of them were so crooked like roofs that they shielded me from the sun as I read. The word and the land were one and the same.

Nights when the moon came out to check the land below were pale and quiet. I liked looking through my bedroom window at the way the moon caressed the few clouds before falling asleep. I liked knowing that the prairie field would always be there. When Sammy moved out of our bedroom, I felt freer to stay up and watch. I used a flashlight to read my books. Sometimes the moon was so strong I didn't need it.

When I saw my father's house after years away, it was a shock to see the prairie land across the road filled with a sea of corn. It wasn't just my mother who'd died; Mrs. Marshall did too. Her kids sold the land for a very good price as the land had been made extremely fertile after having lain fallow for so many years.

Then the house of memory itself: it was no longer a pale blue. It had been repainted white. The garage, too. The barn was still a rusted red, but it wasn't old or anything; it was still in good shape. I didn't see any cows grazing in the pastures. Maybe it was too hot out. I saw some men working the fields, but they seemed to be of darker skin. I wasn't surprised. I had heard about more and more Mexicans migrating up north where there was hard farm work to be found, and I suspected that many of them were illegals. It seemed that hard physical labor was no longer solely the domain and envy of white young men.

I stepped into the house. The kitchen counters and table, and dining room table too, were overflowing with casseroles and . . . so much *food*. Dad said, "That's for after the funeral." Wow. I wouldn't taste Mom's cooking ever again. I held back my tears and walked throughout the house. So much had changed, and yet not much had. *I* was the one who had changed. I couldn't possibly see the house where I grew up the same way again.

When someone doesn't change but you do, who do you think is the ghost here?

The house where I learned to love you has become a stranger too.

On the day I left after Mom's funeral, I felt more hollow than ever. I was an empty shell moving through time and space for no reason at all. There were things I had to do, which I didn't want to do, but society in its illogic had dictated that I must. I'd observed the day before how my brothers held back their tears at the service and the burial in the cemetery on the edge of town, but Sally couldn't stop sobbing. It was as if she'd been burdened with the task of crying for all of us Badamore men. I felt badly for her, and the detachment I'd experienced from it all worried me. Did it mean that I was a bad son, a traitor who'd turned against his own blood? Did it mean that my lack of emotion over the last few days was my way of punishing Mom for choosing cigarettes over me? Did it mean that I'd lost the ability to feel anything? Had I died too?

On the bus I sensed Craig's presence in the empty seat next to me. I looked out the window, watching the farms and fields roll on by. I wanted him to hold my hand, but the air conditioning was warmer than the chill of him breathing the kisses I'd so craved, and I'd longed for them to be disease-free. Of course, I knew that being positive wasn't the death sentence it used to be, but still. What Craig had gone through was forever tattooed on my heart.

In the first winter after Mom died, I took a bus to the farthest stop north in the burbs and walked a few miles beyond the outlet mall into the woods. I didn't know if I was trespassing on private property, but I didn't care. I needed to go deep into the gnarly and rickety thicket of saplings and trees. Maybe I'd find her barely alive, her face blue from negligence and her hands frostbitten from a

lack of affection. Out of her breath would be her last puff of cigarette smoke. When I found her, I'd bend down and perform CPR
on her. I'd jackhammer my oxygen right into her mouth, and
she'd cough back to life. She'd look up into my eyes with such
wonder. She wouldn't be Mom, but the child she used to be before
farm life ruined her enough to accept the ministrations of my father. Her hair was long and flowing like the river she used to play
in when she was young. Her eyes were full of the sun I'd rarely
glimpsed in her while I was growing up. Her laughs were simple
as a cowbell echoing across the pasture. She didn't know who I
was at first. Then she recognized me. "Why did you save me when
I was supposed to be dead?"

"You never saved me when I was alive," I said.

"That's because you never needed any saving. Of all my kids you
were the strongest. You got out while you could. Go. Go be free."

I shook my head no. I unzipped my jacket and wrapped its front
flaps around her. She had shrunk small enough that I could barely
cradle her inside my arms. She rested her chilled face against mine,
and together we trudged through the woods. I didn't know where
we were going, or where we should be going. I wanted to take her
to a warm cabin, but there was none to be found.

As the early evening overtook my steps, I realized that in my
arms was nothing but a dead body. It didn't belong to my mother.

It belonged to me.

I dropped it out of repulsion.

As my other body crashed into the snow, I felt the jolt of ice
hit the same spots that the body of me had touched in the snow.
I screamed. The body didn't move; just lay askew like a Raggedy
Andy doll. I touched my own face to confirm that I was still alive.

Yes, I was.

I turned away, and the longer I moved toward the brightly-lit
parking lot outside the outlet mall, the sharper I felt his breath
seep into the blood circulating through my body. I'd been emotionally dead for a long time, especially after Craig and now this,

but this was ridiculous. I was still alive. I was moving toward my bus stop, and cars did stop to let me through. This meant I wasn't a figment of imagination. I existed.

By the time my bus arrived, I sat by the fogged window. People boarded with their overflowing bags of designer bargains.

As the bus pulled away, I saw in the distance a flicker of shadow. I knew what it was. My dead half was barely alive. Losing Craig had caused him to die, and losing Mom condemned him to the cemetery of my dreams. He needed more than ever my oxygen, my blood. He needed to draw the cigar of my entire soul into himself so he could live. For that to happen, I'd have to die.

Sometimes I felt so drained from the experience that I'd jolt awake to find Mom sitting in an old coat and a wire cart with wobbly wheels filled with all her belongings stashed into a garbage bag. The stench of her smoking addiction would pervade the entire bus, and all of us would be resisting the urge to touch our twitching noses. She turned and stared defiantly at each one of us until we each had to look away and pray that she'd get off the bus soon.

Ghosts are everywhere if we forget how to look for them, and there they rise, from the crypts of our dead memories. When we try to remember their faces more clearly, they crumble into ashes in our hands.

Mom, when you died, your lungs exploded like a balloon pricked with a pin. Its many leaves turned into sheets of paper falling out of spines thickly veined like men's hands being forced to release against their will. The wings flitted high above us until they, full of coos and woos, turned into white doves beating their wings. They filled the sky so much I couldn't see the blue behind their fluttering bodies. When I called out your name, Ida Jean Badamore, the birds whooshed right into a single textbook weighing heavily in my hands. I looked at its cover, which was all white save for the title, *Woman*, in lipstick red. All around me was endless prairie in autumn, in that cusp between harvest and fallow. No road, no tractor, no barn in sight. Not even a lone tree. I opened the book and saw its inner folds of flesh opening wide to fire a thousand and one sperms of fury at me. I felt scalded, and I shivered when the wind turned icy. I felt robbed of speech. I wanted to explain, Mom, that I wasn't the enemy. You were the reason why I'd chosen to minor in Gender Studies, as I felt unable to understand you as a woman. I wanted to understand why you'd long felt inferior, powerless enough not to act on your dreams. I wanted to comprehend just how society had indoctrinated you against the pox of equality. I looked at the book and found its pages blank.

Did you want me to write in it?

Stop saying that I can. I'm not a writer.

No, Mom, I can't. I'm a *man*.

You can't expect me to write the authoritative text about the female experience because I'm a man; after all, heterosexual male privilege has destroyed you. You need to change that way of thinking.

Go haunt not me or another male writer with your stories of woe and wing; go whoosh your wings among the women who know what it feels like to be treated as a second-class citizen yet blessed enough with the compassion for those less than them without romanticizing them with the gift of first-class writing. Let them channel you and impregnate your memory with the music that will outlast your collaborators. The prairie is pure woman, and men have been trying to force it into submission.

You have wings. You are a goddess among the clouds.

Situated on the edge of Laronde, the Eagle used to be a saloon for the down-and-out back in the forties, but it was oddly overlooked during downtown's aggressive urban renewal in the sixties. It stayed shuttered for decades until the mid-eighties when a gay couple bought the building and turned it into what it is today.

During my college years I heard a lot about the Eagle. It was filled with skanky old men in leather outfits, and they were all ugly with saggy tits. It was so filled with cigarette smoke you couldn't breathe. It was a dump with a dingy rainbow flag in front. That's all what it was supposed to be, but I never saw the inside of the place until Craig expressed surprise that I hadn't visited it.

He paid my admission, took my hand, and pulled me into the noisy darkness. It was technically our first date.

Once my eyes were acclimated to the dimness, I saw that it looked like any other tavern I'd seen growing up north. A long mirror behind the counter? Check. A long bar counter with bar stools screwed onto the wooden floor? Check. A TV showing closed-captioned games at both ends of the counter? Check. A CD Wurlitzer jukebox with floating neon pipes throbbing out country songs? Check. But that was where the similarities ended.

No woman was anywhere in sight.

They were all men. They weren't young snobs trying to fit in with designer label clothes or expensive haircuts. They weren't trying to be hip with the latest club music. They weren't dancing just to show how hot and lithe they were. They didn't reek of cologne. Sweat, and the promise of even more, underlined their every movement. They wore T-shirts and jeans. Some of them looked like truckers, scruffy and tired from a long day on the highway. Their boots were lived in, caked with age and abuse.

Others wore leather harnesses across their naked chests and jeans tucked into chaps. Some of them puffed away on cigars. They kept their eyes slightly hidden by the brims of their leather caps. This was in the days before the city passed an anti-smoking ordinance for bars and restaurants.

So much testosterone was packed to the rafters I thought I'd died and gone to heaven. These guys had come from the comic books of my adolescence, but with the novelty of leather accouterments. That, I didn't understand.

"Some guys wear leather because it makes them feel hot," Craig said. "It's like they go into a different mind zone, and they get to be what they really want to be."

He caught my look of puzzlement.

"Look, it's like a cigar. It's big, thick, and manly. You can be a short guy just like me, but when you light one up, you get noticed. They see right away that you're a man. You're sending off signals to everyone that you're man enough to smoke a cigar. Being man enough can really turn some guys on. Leather, cigars, jeans, boots, whatever—it's like an addiction sometimes." He smiled at me. "But me? I'm addicted to you. You're so sweet-tasting."

That night I met some of Craig's friends at the Eagle. I still didn't like the taste of beer, but I hung out on Friday nights once in a while.

Then Craig got sick and died.

I never went back. Just couldn't. Not for a long, long time.

There are still moments in the Eagle when I have those split-second flashbacks of Craig talking with his buddies while I return from the restroom. He was surprisingly easy to spot as he was so short. You don't know truly how much you love someone until you feel how much you miss him.

James, I don't believe in organized religion, but I've prayed to God many times to bring Craig back. Even for just one hour so I could tell him all the things I'd been so afraid to utter out loud when he was alive.

Please don't be so proud like me. You'll regret it to the end of your days.

For Christmas I decided to buy you a few cigars known as the *Perdomo Edicion de Silvio*. I had noted that seemed to be your favorite, so I went down to The Aroma, a fairly large cigar shop six blocks away from work. The front area had comfortable leather chairs and a pile of newspapers. Men of a certain age sat in them and puffed away while they read the papers. My gaydar didn't flash on for any of them, but I liked how they enjoyed their smokes. They seemed wholly at home with themselves.

The silver-haired guy behind the counter was quite debonair with a thick 'stache, its ends curled upward like Frank Morgan's in *The Wizard of Oz*. I didn't know how to pronounce the name of the cigar, so I brought along a piece of paper. "Ah, yes. It's over there." He pointed to the humidor room off to the side. It had wide windows so you could see the shelves of merchandise inside. Up close, I was surprised to see so many different kinds of cigars available. I had no idea. All I'd known was the occasional cigar puffing away in movies, and the kind you'd smoked.

"I don't speak Spanish at all, but could you pronounce the name of the cigar?"

"*Perdomo Edicion de Silvio.*"

"*Per-domo Edicion de Silvio.*"

"No. *Perdomo.*"

I tried again. "*Perdomo.*"

"Yes. Is this a gift for someone?"

I nodded. "It's for my boyfriend." I hadn't meant to say it that way, but James, if a guy is going to spend forty bucks on some cigars on a guy he's having the most passionate sex of his life with, his heart is already hoping to call you "boyfriend." You may not like my line of reasoning, but most people would agree.

The man stepped back an inch.

I didn't smile, but I knew I'd scored a minor triumph. Do you know why, James? He'd assumed that I was straight, so he has to learn that we gay people are everywhere. Money doesn't have a sexual orientation; people do.

"He said that this was his favorite cigar shop, so."

"That's . . . good."

In that moment I wish I had taken a picture of you with my iPhone so I could show him what a hunk you were.

As he rang up the sale, I turned to look closely at the sitting area. There were six plush chairs, three facing the other three. Each had an ashtray set on a knee-high stand, and a reading lamp arching from behind the chair. The side tables had the day's news-papers. Above us were huge ventilators, but they were fairly quiet.

An older man sat with his cigar by the window. The winter light made his skin look quite pale, the haze of smoke from his mouth enveloping his face for a moment such that I couldn't see what he looked like; just his body. He wasn't a tall man, but he had a pronounced belly that strained against his Oxford shirt. For a moment I thought it was you sitting there, not as you now, but as you twenty years from now.

I glanced around the cigar shop and realized that in twenty years, it wouldn't be a big deal for straight men to be smoking their favorite cigars and having amiable conversations with gay men, talking about their women and their men in equal measure. No one would feel threatened. Straight men of a certain build and bulk would take to calling themselves bears, and straight women would identify themselves as bear chasers. Young girls would oooh and ahhh over teen idols labeled as otters. Straight men would realize how much hotter they would be if they stopped shaving their faces every so often. College girls would say they wanted a cub boyfriend, and everyone would know what they meant. And it wouldn't be such a big deal in high school if two football players slow-danced with each other at the prom.

Only time will tell.

Do I believe that ghosts exist? No. There's been much talk of people experiencing visions of spectral beings, but I think it's a figment of their imaginations. Sometimes they experience some-thing so intense that words fail them, and the concept of an ap-parition is the next best description. Ghosts appear and reappear, revealing the state of our minds at the time like a mirror back to us. We feel the chill of recognition, and we say we've just seen a ghost when it's always been us all along.

Craig still haunts me from time to time. I know that if he were alive, he would be sleeping right here beside me. He was a major cuddler, and I liked that about him. He may have been very short, but he felt of the right height when he wrapped his arms around me. His legs draped all over my thighs, leaving my feet free. I liked that. Those nights when nothing moved except the sighing of our chests I felt as if our arms, hands, fingers would burst forth into vines budding and expanding and weaving in and out of each other until we were inseparable. It was scary to feel that, and yet so wonderful.

When he died, my entire trunk was chopped apart and left to rot. I had no branches, no roots. I was a stump ripped out and wood-chipped into pieces. My heart was squished with slugs that couldn't get enough of the pit blackness of rage at the injustice of death. I was no longer a young man with a worthless MFA; I was an old man with nothing to show for his heart and his art. I flitted like a plastic bag in the wind, hoping to hook a tree branch so I could hang on and not float away to the cemetery of the forgotten stumps. But no one was having me. I was good enough for a fuck, but too ethereal to keep.

I said I was grieving.

I said I was a widower.

I said I wasn't ready to date.

I said I wasn't ready for a relationship.

What I never said was: Mr. Loneliness is my husband, and I can't divorce him right now. Just can't.

Then you appeared and beckoned me into your truck, house, bed. It was the most wonderful affair of my life. Not once did I miss my husband on those weekends. I saw how miserable he was, but I didn't care. I was tired of being miserable. He was always annoyingly right whenever we argued.

I cheated on my husband so recklessly that I was due for payback.

Did he tell you that he'd never divorce me as long as I lived because he'd married me first?

Then I realize Mr. Loneliness is the biggest bigamist alive. He will marry anyone who'll have him and break their hearts. Divorcing him will be the hardest thing they'll go through. Remember, he's your husband too.

The wind of loneliness is what propels ghosts to sing silences and suddenly vanish. The gusts of chill play tricks on the mind's eye of our bodies until we think our bodies are seeing what we were afraid to see in our own mirrors. We are transparent; we float; we sigh endlessly. We turn into oceans that are smaller than a drop of rain, and we are perpetually falling from the sky, waiting to splash on something concrete but the earth below is too far away. How we long to crash and feel the lightning jolt of pain, just to know that we aren't figments of our own imaginations. Let us bleed so we can exist.

The kisses we shared have turned into gray curls of smoke. They float away, sometimes dropping back to tease me, and they rise up just out of my reach.

When Craig died, I felt I couldn't love again. I didn't see the point. And what's more, one night at the Eagle some years ago I overheard three guys standing by the wall over there, right near where I saw you for the first time. I didn't know who they were at the time, but they were all very hot. Each one of them was a veritable stud; they wouldn't be lying if they said they were VGL in their online profiles. Most of them wore leather armbands on their left biceps to show that they were tops. They wore leather caps, and they groomed their facial hair. One man in particular had a beard that was so black one wondered if it was actually dark blue. I couldn't tell, but his eyes were brown as chestnut. I was in lust.

Of course, he didn't know I existed. He acted as if most of us didn't. He was there to revel in his own hotness and to remind everyone that he was too hot for them. It's an ego trip of the worst kind. Still, I couldn't tear myself away from looking. Until I met you, I thought he was the most perfect specimen of manhood

I'd ever laid my eyes on. I never overheard his name. I stood over there, unsure whether I should ask for another glass of ginger ale, when I noticed him talking with his buddies. They were pointing out this and that guy lining the bar and elsewhere while talking with each other.

He said, "Had him, had him, had him . . ."

The other said, "Had him, had him . . ."

I felt sickened. What was this? Had the bear community become an arena of sexual sports where it was all about statistics?

I didn't want to be just another number, another notch on someone's bedpost.

Uh-*huh*.

That's why I didn't come back to another bear event for a long time. Years, actually.

I went online instead and discovered that many bears had felt rejected at bear events. It was no surprise that a few bear events were cancelled in recent years when there weren't enough RSVPs. The bears do not treat their own kind very well.

Bears online told me stories. Oh, a lot of stories.

One told me how he went to a bear party at Jolt, a bar that used to be on Speck Street. He was of Scandinavian descent, so he was naturally blond. He had been so excited to learn about the bear community, so he showed up. He didn't know anyone there, but within five minutes of his arrival, he overheard two guys shouting into each other's ears over the loud music: "Look at that Swede! We gotta fuck him first before anybody does!"

He turned around, and he never went back. He hangs out online because he feels safer. I don't blame him. Do you? What kind of a community are we if we keep rating each other on fuckability? Quite astonishing, actually, when considering that so many of us were often overweight growing up. I'm sure we've been picked on because of our weight, and we have to turn around and reject anyone we deem unattractive, or reduce them to potential cum receptacles? Are they remotely aware of what they're doing to each other and to themselves?

You shrugged every time I brought this up. "So?" you said. "It's just the way things are."

Oh, really? What about your missing foot?

Surely people had to have freaked when they saw it. Did they ever make an effort to maintain their distance from you? Did they avert their eyes from yours in the elevator? Or did they tell you how amazing and inspiring you were to move around with your prosthetic foot, which was really a passive-aggressive reminder of how superior they still were to you?

Did you ever want to tell them to shut the fuck up?

Did you ever want to look them in the eye and say, "Well?"

Did you ever want to shout at everyone to stop looking at you like a freak?

One of the reasons why I loved you so much was the fact that you didn't want pity. You didn't become an alcoholic or a junkie when you lost your foot. It must've been a hard adjustment, but you were a man. You were still that tough quarterback out on the field, and you were playing the last home game of the season. You were set on winning, and you did. You scored a lot of touchdowns with me, many more than you'll ever know.

You taught me not to pity anyone because they were different. They were still people. I've never forgotten that.

All I want is one more chance to tell you all the things I've always wanted to tell you but had felt too scared to share. I'm tired of dreaming the conversations we will never have.

I will never forget the taste of your sweat and smoke. Some nights, when I'm not thinking of anything at all, it all comes back. I inhale as much as I can, which is ridiculous since the memory is not contained anywhere in my nasal cavity, but embedded deep somewhere in my brain. I only have to close my eyes and gently pull in the draw of you until I breathe nothing else. I jack off this cigar of mine right here on this lonely bed of mine, and when I finally smoke out, I know it's because it's the only way my body can grieve for you.

Each puff of cum is a tear, a pearl.

Sometimes I wish I could move like an invisible spirit through the Eagle on Friday nights, but I'm afraid to join the army of ghosts still floating inside, overhearing the animated conversations of their friends, still alive, as they drink their cheap beers. For them it's always Happy Hour.

I don't want to hear what these ghosts want more than anything to say, because I know that they'll say the same thing: *I still love you I miss you so much I can't bear to leave here and say good-bye to all my friends.* Even though I know the bar is air-conditioned when I step inside on hot summer nights, that initial chill always makes me think of those whose names I'll never know. They're still crowding the place even on nights when it's dead. I feel their eyes everywhere, but I don't mind that actually. They are men who've had sex with other men, so they know what it's like to want to just fuck this or that hot stranger, to explore boundaries of kink, and to ache for a deeper connection with someone who's unfortunately chosen someone else. And of course, there's the camaraderie. They don't judge each other for what they like to do with their cocks and balls. They just are: bar buddies, platonic good friends, potential tricks, and married but not dead husbands in open relationships.

The living have so many possibilities to choose from, and the dead have only one possibility. They simply don't want to leave. They are too in love with the memory of their younger selves. Doesn't matter that the men they'd loved back then have gotten old, or that a few of them now require pills to sustain their erections. They snuggle against these beautiful men, who will remain forever young in their doomed eyes, and try not to weep from too much happiness. When these dead men were alive, they hadn't wanted much else, and now, here in the chapel of the Eagle, they can continue to pay their respects.

James, you must've known how badly I wanted to pay my respects to you. I wanted to stand next to you on that barstool and rest my head on your sturdy shoulder while you shot the breeze with your buddies. Sometimes you would give me a kiss on the lips when you caught the look of expectancy in my eyes. Everyone would know that I was yours and yours alone, and that would make me feel so proud.

What have I done to make you feel so ashamed of me?

What?

Tell me.

I dreamed I was a somnambulist, walking with eyes closed and yet never bumping into walls or tripping over curbs. Somehow the further I walked, the more my clothes melted and faded away from my body as I walked the miles and miles along the cinder-filled shoulders of a loud highway until I turned right and right again until up the hill and down the road was your house. Awakening, I was startled naked as a skeleton. Chill snapped at the very flesh inside my bones. Moonlight, caked of embers, lit the deep indentations of my ribcage. There on the road was a half-finished cigarette. I shivered; I thought I was going to topple over, but I picked it up. It still had a faint glow, emitting my mother's death breath, as I inhaled. Just then you opened the door, a shadow beckoning me into the fireplace of your house. Felt like centuries before I finally arrived on your steps, but arrive I did.

Sometimes I dream of being a cigarette.

Isn't that funny, James? You said you were a cigarette smoker for twelve years until one night a buddy offered you a good cigar of his to try. Cigars eventually weaned you off cigarettes altogether.

I want to be the last cigarette you missed. You'd light me up and inhale me, storing each puff of memory deep into the chamber of your lungs. I would stuff each bronchiole of yours with cotton balls of want and need to the point where the only way you could breathe would be through me, my perfect set of lungs.

I am pure scent. I am the weight of smoke sinking into each fiber of fabric and seeping into your skin.

Each inhalation and exhalation is a confession of love and lust.

You make me confess so easily.

I am a puff, a poem.

You would never see me as a poem, but I am one. It's a question of mastering each puff for the most intense release. I will hold off as long as I can until the last line will make you erupt so many times you've lost count.

Our first night together was the most sublime poetry reading ever, and no one was there to hear us. How so beautiful is that, and how that is so beautiful.

I don't write poetry anymore. That stuff feels so juvenile now, but each time we kissed and made love, I felt as if I was writing a new poem, only to have it disappear, and to find it rewritten in startling ways. Then they all evaporated into thin air. No recordings, no applause.

You didn't just make a man out of me.

You made a dream poet out of me.

Of you I shall sing in my dreams, and only you will hear my songs when I play the lyre of your cock. Your sweat is honey, and your cum is milk. On both I shall subsist, for they are the stuff of nicotine most sublime.

Come inhale me while I'm still alive. I am that flame flickering in your breath before I touch the tip of your cigarette. Let me light up the dark recesses of your soul. Let me cast aside shadows to find the most brilliant coals and free yourself of darkness. Let me blow songs into your lungs so you can find the power of wind coursing through your veins.

Come exhale me when I'm dead, and you would know that you have been loved. You would know that each night when you sleep, and each morning when you jack off, someone has loved you. You would know all this without knowing why.

I am both ash and wind, but I'm still here. Come blow me away in that polar vortex of your tentative affections, and I will return in the spring with my dandelion whiskers. I will sow my seed everywhere, and when my children burst forth in yellow, you would know that I have never forgotten you.

FOOTPRINTS TURNED EMBER IN SNOW

> The heart of another is a dark forest, always, no
> matter how close it has been to one's own.
> —*Willa Cather*

I've thought many times of renting a car and coming north to your house and knocking on your door for an explanation, but I thought that would make me too creepy-stalkerish.

Instead, in dreams I remain an ether floating through your kitchen. I'm made of transparent ice, a sheet of glass that never reflects anything even in broad daylight.

It hurts that you don't even notice me.

You sit alone in the kitchen, eating a microwaved dinner. You look out the window and see the road. Very few cars pass by at this time of evening.

It's the kind of country where everyone goes to bed early. The darkness is that powerful.

The radio by the stove is on. It's not loud, but it's enough. News about politics and entertainment scratch the air.

You like the silences. Very comforting.

It's a fur coat on your shoulders. It weighs heavily on you, but it gives you that semblance of surefootedness. You wear it well.

You scrape the plastic box for the last of mashed potatoes and gravy.

You let out a deep sigh of satisfaction.

I want to come closer to you and kiss your head, but you are too hot like the sun. If I came closer, the fire of you would melt the ice of me.

This is why ghosts don't like to stay long when they visit.

The way you and I rolled on top of each other, over each other, laughing when we felt each other's fingers tickling our sides, our feet, rolling across the carpet in front of your TV, our laughs turning hoarse from too much, we couldn't give enough tickles, we had to stop laughing, it was way too much really, then we stopped. You lay on your back and looked at me; you looked different, almost childlike. The afternoon sun glowed in the boyishness of your face. I saw the white roots of your beard about to gleam. I kissed you on the lips, and you kissed me back. We'd fallen off the sofa quite by accident after a movie—Frank Capra's *It Happened One Night* with Clark Gable and Claudette Colbert—had finished. You said that it was a real shame that Carole Lombard had turned down Ms. Colbert's part, especially when Mr. Gable could've fallen in love with her sooner and married her just as quickly, and I jabbed you on the elbow. "Carole Lombard is not the goddess you think she is." I'd jabbed you so hard that you nearly fell off the sofa. "Sorry!"

You then pulled me off the sofa, and I nearly crashed onto your chest, but you were too quick for me. You tickled me, and without thinking, I tickled you right back. We whooped with laughs, it was as if we were free to let go; we gasped, guffawed when we felt an unexpected tickle.

Then it was all over. Another movie on the Turner Classic Movies channel had begun, but we didn't look up at the TV. Our eyes, full of light—wasn't it sunlight? It had to be. Somehow we'd captured a beam of light, unfiltered yet tender, into the cavern of our souls, shining us from within, and we cocooned into each other. We snuggled, two puzzle pieces fitting perfectly, there on the carpet. I placed my head on your chest and listened to your heart, a drum banging softly in search of a song. I closed my eyes and hummed a song I didn't know; a made-up tune much like how a child would spout scales of silly sounds out of a happy boredom. We melted into silence, and then without preamble, you lifted my chin and kissed me, tasting me all over again. We fell into our blissfully familiar rhythms right there on the carpet, and we shuddered over and over again. Your body quaked so violently that you nearly collapsed on top of me, but you caught yourself in time. Your hands on the carpet held you up as you stared into my eyes as your hips thrust uncontrollably.

Do you remember any of that, James? You made me believe; gave me hope that we could make a Hollywood movie of our own, only that it would be called *It Happened One Afternoon*.

A week or so after you hung up on me, Mom's ghost came to visit me in my bedroom. I was on my side, trying to sleep; this was before I had to ask my doctor for some Ambien. She sat opposite me. I couldn't quite pinpoint her features, but at least she wasn't coughing like she did when she was alive. She stared at me and said nothing. I couldn't figure out why she'd bothered to come. I wanted to ask her questions, but there was nothing I could ask her. She was never comfortable with talking about sex, let alone heartbreak.

For a time we stared at each other.

Then she crossed her arms.

I crossed mine.

Her face softened.

I whispered, "Mom?"

She evaporated.

The room felt filled up with ice. A moment later, it felt as if on fire. I was confused. I got up and went to the bathroom. I had gotten a fever. I took my temperature. I was 101 degrees. I soaked a washcloth under cold water and put it on my forehead. I tried to sleep. I took my temperature again. Still 101 degrees. I heated up some chicken noodle soup and filled it with oyster crackers. Sleep. Nothing.

You rose above me like Michelangelo's God from the Sistine Chapel.

You didn't wear the white robe that many painters of yore always used to depict the white-bearded God. You were naked, and your cock and balls floated as if in zero gravity. You darted from one end of my bedroom to another, all the while keeping your eyes on me. You lifted your arms and put your hands behind your head. You knew how much this display of mass and muscle had turned me on. You winked at me and floated right down to me.

Together we'd rise up to the heavens and fuck all of the night and the day too. Everyone would hear us, but we wouldn't care. We were gods, reborn with a new strength. Holding hands, we'd never let each other go.

My alarm clock suddenly buzzed.

I didn't know where I was for a moment.

I thought I was floating, but instead I was dead weight on the limp raft of a bed. I was floating nowhere. The stars of your eyes vanished into the black.

I took my temperature. My fever had broken. I called in sick, and I slept a perfect death.

It was night when I did at last awaken. My room shone like the cosmos. There were no walls; just stars breathing everywhere. It was the most beautiful sight I'd ever seen. I felt I mattered, even if I were much smaller than an atom and far more inconsequential in the larger scheme of the universe.

I wept.

It's such a long, long voyage home, and I've no compass but my heart to guide my way. You are my true north.

One night I'd felt again like a somnambulist, traversing between dusk and dawn, in a city that looked suspiciously like Paris but wasn't. The streets were cobblestoned, the streetlamps gas-lit and the fog heavy. I walked slowly, afraid to bump into strangers, all wearing long black coats and shiny shoes, dragging their feet past me out of the fog. Still, as gray as the air was, I searched their eyes. They were disinterested in me. I didn't know where I should be going; I was simply lost. My feet felt like concrete, yet wings were anchored to my back. I could feel the muscles in my back flexing my wings. I could fly at any time I wanted to, but in order for that to happen, I would have to cut off my feet.

I turned to look at myself in the glass of yet another sad café. No one was sitting in there; it was all lit but completely empty. It's as if ghosts, invisible to the human eye, had taken up residence in the café, and only I knew this fact. Then I noticed in my reflection that the color of my clothes was black. I couldn't discern the contours of my heavy fabrics, the drape of my long coat. I dragged closer to the window-glass and peered into the great emptiness inside. An utter chill tiptoed up and down my spine. I noticed a few more black-suited men and black-dressed women straggling past behind me. I realized with a startle that I was a mourner like them. I had come to mourn the death of us. I turned and followed these people into a large cathedral where a choir was singing a dirge. Up in the air were coffins, floating like balloons full of helium without bumping into each other. We mourners gazed upon the fantastic sight, and it was then I noticed that we each had a pair of wings, shimmering like a raven's.

The singing soon stopped.

In the distance a somber-voiced priest, decked out in red, spoke quietly, yet with an iron authority, from the bare altar. He swung a censer filled with incense and walked up and down the aisles around our pews. The coffins rose higher and higher until they touched the stone-carved beams holding up the roof. The priest did not seem perturbed by this. We mourners turned to each other, our faces asking the same question: would these coffins push up against the roof and let it tumble to the earth, shattering into fatal chunks?

The priest returned to the altar.

The singing resumed.

The sunbeams, colored by stained glass in the windows, coasted to our faces until the wrinkles of worry fell away. It was as if the sharp edges of our years had been smoothened out with an inch of freshly fallen snow.

The coffins dropped slowly. They did not dance or sway. They were pulleyed down by invisible ropes.

The singing stopped.

The coffins in that precise moment opened, exploding not into splinters of wood or corpses falling out, but into a mad flurry of doves. They spun around each other for a moment before they headed toward the back entrance and out into the air.

Also in that same moment we felt the savage ripping of our wings from our backs. It happened so quickly we didn't have a chance to cry out. The wings, blackened with blood, floated upward like tiny feathers into the mist of the coffin remains. We heard the distinct sound of coffin lids clamping shut.

The singing resumed, but not with a lamentation.

We discovered that our feet were indeed light, no longer stiff from dragging for so long. The black wings which had marked us into the purgatory of grief had been linked to our feet. The sun outside turned stronger, so strong that our black clothes grew into the color of flowers blooming. We burst forth into peals of laughter, and we began dancing in the aisles. The singers by then had begun their rhythmic clapping as they sang of joy. No more darkness, they reminded us.

I am still awaiting that moment of utter exhilaration, the freedom of never thinking about you again, but I just can't. You have coffined my heart, and I have no idea where you've buried me.

Three weeks before Christmas, you said you'd pick me up at work after Happy Hour at the Eagle. But after a truly exhausting day, I didn't want to wait around at work. The monotonous smell of coffee was getting to me. I called you, but you didn't pick up the phone. I left a voicemail, and I walked over to the Eagle with my weekend bag. I thought I'd have a ginger ale and pretend not to know you while you hung out with your buddies. I figured I'd see you leave, and I'd follow you. Or I'd step outside on the smoking patio and call you if you weren't there.

I tried not to watch you.

I saw your buddies gathered around by the counter. You weren't drinking beer like your buddies were. I thought that was strange. Didn't Happy Hour mean cheap drinks?

Then you caught sight of me. No flicker of recognition.

Off to the side was a huge cardboard box piling up with teddy bears donated for charity. They wanted all sorts of toy donations for the tots, but it seemed that everyone had only teddy bears to give away. I wanted to dive into the box and drown and scream where no one could hear me. Hadn't I deserved better treatment after two months together?

After I finished my drink, I knew what I had to do. I wouldn't spend that weekend with you. I waited for you to glance my way again, and when you finally did, I gave you a look of disgust that startled you.

I smiled to myself when I saw you recomposing your stoic face.

I didn't look back when I went to the coat check and picked up my bag. I was going to go home, go online, and go out for a hook-up. I wanted to have the sleaziest sex with anybody and forget all about you, what a prick you were, what the fuck was I thinking?

It was snowing outside the bar when I adjusted my backpack.

I didn't think you were going to call me, but you did.

"So you think you can give me attitude?" I didn't even say hello. "Fuck you."

"Hey," you said. "I'm sorry."

"I don't buy that. You wanna apologize?"

You said nothing.

"I come back in there, and you're going to give me the longest kiss of your life in front of everybody."

You hung up.

I stared at the phone for a long moment, and I put it away.

Fine. Be that way. Whatever.

It was going to be a long walk home. I pulled out my hat and started walking south to my neighborhood.

"Hey."

I turned around. "I got a name, you know."

"Bill, come back here."

"No. *You* come right here."

You looked furious when you walked close to me. You weren't wearing a jacket! "You want a fucking kiss? Okay." You kissed me on the lips right there as cars passed us by.

I was so surprised. It took me a moment before I could say, "Apology accepted."

"Good. I'll be right back."

I stood outside the Eagle, waiting for you. It seemed like forever, but it was probably five minutes. You returned with your leather jacket. There was something lost in your eyes. I wanted to say something to make you feel better, but I realized I had no words to describe what I'd seen. I wasn't sure if I was able to translate that language of loss.

Instead we stayed silent on our way to your house.

There was no passion between us when we made love that night.

I had become a duty.

I felt worse than shit.

A duty was the last thing I wanted to be.

When you finally fell asleep, I got up and sat on the sofa. I couldn't sleep next to you. I had hurt you. But I knew that for our relationship—if that was what we had—to work, there needed to be more give-and-take, more yin and yang. Everything had been all about you, and you had been taking from me all along.

Yet I felt so guilty and torn up about wanting to take from you.

I wanted to apologize, but how?

I had seen the disgust on your face when I kissed your body as before. Had I become a sexual bore? Or had the party ended already?

When you finally ejaculated, there was no deep-gutted grunt. It was a perfunctory orgasm, the kind that you have on some mornings when you're not exactly super horny but you jack off as something to do before you get out of bed.

I didn't know what I should do. I didn't have a car, and I knew I couldn't very well ask you to take me back to the city that same night.

You walked around the bed and lifted the window a little.

You sat down on the bed; didn't look at me. You took off your prosthetic foot and pulled the blanket over us.

I was so afraid of looking at you that I had to get out of the bedroom.

I felt like such a little shit. What the hell had I done wrong?

Time felt like nothing. I felt as if I was floating in your living room, only that there wasn't any way for me to get out of the house. I felt as if I was tripping, but I wasn't on drugs. I wanted to say how sorry I was, and leave. I sat down on the sofa and wrapped the afghan blanket around my shoulders. I was starting to shiver.

Then you stood naked in the doorway. "Hey."

"What?"

"It'll be okay." You beckoned me to my feet. "Let's get some sleep."

When I slipped beside you, I hesitated. Was there something I should say?

Then you patted my arm and turned onto your side as was your habit.

I cried.

I don't think you ever heard me. It was the quietest cry of my life. I didn't want to wake you up; didn't want to worry you; I didn't want you to be angry at me anymore.

It was then I thought of Craig, and I hadn't thought of him in a long time. I felt his presence, but I couldn't pinpoint him like I usually did.

I dreamed he had slipped behind my back and wrapped his chilly arms around me while I snuggled a little closer to your back. I was forever torn, my dreams made of haze and gauze, between love and death.

The next morning you surprised me when I found you sucking my cock. It was usually you who'd take my hand and place it on your erection first. It was then I knew things between us would be all right again. I shot volumes when I gazed into your eyes as you engulfed me, never letting up, never letting me go.

In the beginning of our weekends together, I talked a lot. I was nervous. I didn't know what else to do. I hadn't felt comfortable with your silences, but I learned to trust that you were still interested. After all, you were the one who'd always made the call and who'd driven down to the city and picked me up.

The last few weekends together we didn't talk much. There wasn't any need to, or it was because I'd sensed that if I did, you'd pull further away from me. With each progressive weekend together, silence became your de facto answer to everything. If you spoke, it was with ecstatic moans and grunts.

I ended up knowing so little about you.

The gaps in your background have vested you with power. A famous photo editor said he preferred photographs with a bit of shadow in them. With that bit of mystery within the frame, we had to strain our eyes a bit more to look into such dark areas for clues that weren't there as wont our human nature, our quest for knowledge. We had been tricked into staring at a photograph a bit longer than a photograph that hid nothing.

Had you tricked me?

Or was I the future you were afraid would come take the familiar night away from your hands, render you powerless like the helpless larvae plucked out of the soil at dawn? My heart is not a bird. My heart has sprung forth from the land itself, the same earth on which you and I stand. Could you feel it rumble like an earthquake, right along the San Andreas Fault of my heart, shaking the foundation of your house miles away? Shake, shake harder. Wake up from the lull of your past. My heart, made of many layers of geological stories, is full of tremors. I am the nightmare of seismology.

My bed when I try to sleep is filled with aftershocks of you. Let the sky fall into shards. Let me be your umbrella.

You said you didn't want to go anywhere for New Year's Eve. No time for that party-hearty. You didn't want anyone around for Christmas either. You didn't venture an explanation.

Still, I'd gotten you those cigars for Christmas, which sat in my closet. Maybe I was being too hopeful.

That day I decided to walk all over the city. A bit of snow had fallen, but it wasn't enough to stop traffic dead in its tracks. The snow was light and puffy. It reminded me of dandelion whiskers, ready to scatter with each stamp of foot on the sidewalk. There weren't many cars, so I felt a bit at peace. The city felt different when it was quiet with its stores closed. It was beautiful.

I thought about watching a movie on my laptop, but when I realized I was only three blocks away from the Eagle, I decided what the hell. I figured the bar would be dead.

I couldn't be more wrong. There were a lot of guys I hadn't seen before. They had apparently come from out of town to visit their relatives. I saw Ted, a guy I'd dated once in college when he was quite skinny, but we discovered to our embarrassment we weren't sexually compatible. I detoured around the bar to the smoking patio outside to see if there was anyone I knew.

I was surprised to find you standing there all by yourself. You were in jeans and a leather jacket, puffing away on a cigar. "What are you doing here? I thought you wanted to spend Christmas alone."

"I changed my mind."

"You could've called me."

You shook his head. "No. I didn't want to mess up your Christmas."

"I've been alone all day. I thought you knew my dad doesn't want me around."

You closed your eyes briefly. "Oh, right. Sorry."

"Wanna come over to my place? You've never seen my room. Besides, I'd love to introduce you to my housemates."

"No. Not tonight." You kept glancing at the entrance. It was as if you were afraid that others would catch us talking.

"Were you expecting somebody?"

"No. Just . . ." You looked at me. "I just need to be alone. Okay?"

I nodded.

When I left, I thought for sure that we'd never meet again. If you had officially broken up with me, I think I'd have been okay with it.

I was very surprised when you called me later that week on Friday morning. "Wanna come up for the weekend?"

"Um, I didn't think . . . well, here's the thing. I didn't think you were going to call me again so I decided to work all weekend."

"Oh."

"I can't read your mind. You have to tell me in advance. A lot of people don't like my boss, so they quit. I'm the one who has to put out fires all the time."

You said nothing.

"You still there?"

"Yeah."

"If you wanna get together for New Year's . . ."

"No. I'll call you later."

You called me again the following Wednesday, two days early. "You free this weekend?"

"Yes."

On our ride up north, I wanted so much to hold your hand and tell you that you were all right. I was filled with a great sadness. Were you going to break up with me then? I couldn't tell, and I didn't want to know.

Yet the sex that night was mind-blowing.

It dawned on me that you were trying to tell me things. You spoke in the tongue of silences, and I moaned. The rhythms of our hands and bodies in sync were beautiful.

I felt all right with the world. I thought we'd survived this horrible misunderstanding.

Then the gas heat went out the next morning. You didn't know how low your cylinder of propane gas had gotten, so you cursed yourself. You made a few phone calls.

I tried to appease you in between calls while you leafed through an old copy of the *Yellow Pages*. I was surprised that anyone still used them.

You waved me away.

By then, we were both wearing many layers. My nose felt like an ice cube.

We stayed in your warmed-up truck and listened to the radio for a long while, waiting for the delivery man. You had to pay extra for same-day delivery.

Finally, the truck showed up. The lanky delivery guy simply rolled the barrel around your house. He asked you if you'd turned off the connection to the tank from inside the house. You went inside, and you hollered through the window. It didn't take him long to replace the empty barrel and roll it back to his truck.

You didn't make conversation. You just watched us through the window.

The delivery guy didn't pay you much attention. He had a long brown beard. He wore an oversized snowmobile jacket, an old pair of jeans, and the tan-orange Red Wing boots. I hadn't seen anyone wear those in a long time. He reminded me of my hometown. He grinned goofily at me whenever you looked away.

I couldn't figure out why until it hit me. He was attracted to me! Not you—*me!* I couldn't believe it.

There was no way I could be hotter than you.

But he didn't glance at you. I don't know if it was because you were standing there with a glum face or because he didn't like your size. I didn't care. Someone had actually found me attractive.

I smiled back.

"You from around here?"

"No. I'm from the city. I'm just staying with James."

"Hey. You can turn it back on," he yelled out to you.

"Got it!" You disappeared from the window. "Done!"

He nodded acknowledgment at you, and he pocketed his tools as he looked at me. "Well. See you later."

You came outside. "Thanks." You tipped him a ten from your wallet.

While we waited for the house to heat up again, you turned to me. "Don't do that to him."

"What? What are you talking about?"

"You were looking at him. Don't be so obvious."

"What? He was obvious about looking at me."

"He can't be gay."

"My gaydar went orange alert on him."

"Just—just don't."

"Are you jealous?"

"No, I'm not."

I harrumphed.

Don't you remember that conversation?

I sure do. If you hadn't cared one way or another, we wouldn't have had that conversation. It was because of that delivery guy I chose to stay with you.

That night you held me a bit longer than usual, and it was then time for you to pull away and sleep. I dreamed of us standing together in tuxedos in a church and holding hands as a minister intoned words: "You are now husbands. You may now kiss each other." You swooped me into your arms and kissed me in front of everyone. I looked up into your eyes, and they were so full of emotion. You were suddenly conversant in the language of eyes. You did love me!

I felt like Irene in *My Man Godfrey* when she realized that Godfrey had to be in love with her even after he's doused her with a sudden shower. She ran around the house, saying, "He loves me, he loves me, he loves me!"

Instead I had to content myself with a deep sleep.

The next morning it seemed as if you'd changed back to the old gruff James. What had happened in your dreams? You never said.

Through the winding forest of yonder, just beyond where you lived, I rode a horse of many spots. It was a fine draft horse, constructed of impressively thick hindquarters and sturdy legs. From the way it moved, surely and nimbly in spite of its brute bulk, I knew it loved me. It chose our path well, for it did not go where branches would nick my face. I could close my eyes and rest my head on its neck, and it would not dare nudge me awake as it carried me through the mottled shade. I felt the full bask of summer hold me close, much like the way my first love did, yes, he did hold me close and not let me go even in the first blink of dawn, and I inhaled the cologne of musk and sweat as I bobbed, a happy child in overgrown clothes, with its mane tickling my nose with each trot. But it did not awaken me at all for I felt blanketed. Then it stopped. It began to breathe heavily. I scratched my eyes open and saw through the fog before us the opening, the private place of self-worship where you let loose the incense of cigar, of trees broken and grayed in the snuff of coal. I tried not to cough on the remaining wisp of acrid smoke still arising from the ground. What had died? The fog slowly lifted its veil, and there you were on the ground before the remains of the log where you liked to sit, the skeleton of you lying with your hands behind your skull, I knew it was you, it had to be you, the bones for your right foot were missing. I screamed, and the fog dropped like sandbags around us until it was heavy with night. No moon, no stars, no wind. Pure black. Not even a sound anywhere. My dear horse began to buck, whinnying like angry whistles; then it shot straight ahead, not caring whether the branches were too low for me. I held on fiercely, like my fingers gripping the edge of ledge sixty stories above pavement, with blood weeping out of my eyes. My horse's name is Melancholia, and it won't let me get off.

In the aftermath of your last phone call, everyone wondered out loud if spring was ever going to arrive. I looked out at the gray skies when I wasn't busy behind the counter. It was full of clouds, and I thought of the way your cigar smoke had cast a spell over me. Your breath, flavored with not only you but the alchemy of tobacco leaves hung to dry and then rolled, flowed like a river rushing upstream into my nose until I couldn't smell anything else but you.

When I closed my eyes, I felt the walls of my coffeehouse around us pull away and the winds rushing in to cradle the two of us off your bed. Our tongues couldn't, wouldn't stop tasting each other. As we floated up, I felt the gentle sprinkle of snow, not cold but warm as kisses, dance around our bodies. Our hands kept moving all over each other as we puffed on each other's tongue, and our exhalations of smoke and oxygen arose like question marks and exclamation points rolled into one. Zero gravity made us only giddy, and our erections glistened as we looped around each other. Below us were your house and the great stretch of land beyond.

We coasted through the woods right into that special clearing of yours. Even though we were naked, we didn't feel a hint of chill. The furnace of love deep in the pits of our souls had been churning out so much heat that even in a land of ice, our tongues tasted only of fire. I floated a moment above you before I landed gently on your chest. I heard the thunder of your heart beating, and I saw the lightning of fear in your eyes.

You suddenly pushed me off you, and I sailed backward through the sky.

I didn't take my eyes off you. Oh, what had I done to you?

The snowflakes that had felt like warm kisses had turned into sandpapery gravel spitting all over my body.

You lay there, unmoving.

I landed a few miles away.

Even though I was shivering to my sure death, I plodded on through the snow back to you. The trees turned its backs against me, and the winds whipped daggers across my body until my bleeding formed into icicled scabs. Still, I felt the fire of you burning away deep inside me.

When I finally got into the clearing, I found you dead. You had turned into blue marble. You'd crossed your arms across your chest. I was afraid to touch your chest as it was covered with ice. It would surely peel away the last layer of skin off my palms. Shivering and feeling ready to go blind, I gazed upon your face. A tear, steaming hot from my eye, dribbled down and splattered across your lips.

The film of ice that had shellacked your body melted, and it didn't stop melting until you'd become a life raft upon which I floated. The waves kept rising, spreading so far out that we were the only people bobbing on the great sea of nowhere. The sun of dawn rose up in the east, and it was then you'd finally opened your eyes.

You smiled and leaned up for a kiss.

When our lips met, we felt suckered into a quicksilver storm of waves gushing higher than buildings, but we were safe inside an invisible bubble. As we rolled in the roiling of sea and storm, we laughed. Nothing could hurt us now. We had the crazy notion of making love no matter what, and that was what we did. We moaned, screamed, ejaculated over and over again. Together we were invincible.

Then the winds stopped raging.

We floated on the waves, which were dropping like gravity.

We held on to each other as the water seeped quickly into the parched earth.

When our bubble touched the mud, it cracked. We were lucky that its shards didn't cut our skin.

We got up, and we walked hand in hand across the renewed land. We followed the evening sun, back into the dark forest behind your house, and it was then we'd lost touch with each other. We'd become ghosts, unable to kiss again no matter how much we wanted to. The chill of your presence shielding the flame of your heart turned me into ice.

Some nights I awaken, wondering if I've become an ice statue.

One February weekend the windchill dropped to thirty-three below zero. Your house was a bit drafty, which you hadn't much minded, but this time you kept the bedroom window firmly closed. You piled two more quilts on top of the bed. It was so cold that I left my T-shirt and long johns and socks on. But you? You had to stay completely naked. I couldn't believe it. The fur on your body felt knitted, yes, but I didn't think it was enough to keep you warm.

Under the heavy blankets, you pulled me close to you, and you didn't push me away after a few moments. I rested my head on your chest, right over your heart.

I nearly cried when I could hear your heartbeat so clearly. I breathed in your sweaty and furry scent. You made me nearly drunk.

Somehow in the middle of my cautious breathing, you kissed me softly on the head.

Don't you remember doing that? I think you were afraid of jolting me awake.

By the time I woke up, you had already showered and dressed for the day.

Never thought of how you'd cuddled me until now, not until I wrapped my arms around my big fat pillows and pretended they were you that I was holding, resting my face against your flannelled back and closing my eyes. In our last month together, you took to cuddling me for longer than just a few minutes, each time longer than the previous night. I never timed the duration of your cuddles, but I remember thinking how odd you were to make the first move by wrapping your arms around me, pulling me close. You must've known you were going to let me go; it was just a question of when. If that was the case, how cruel, how savage you were! You didn't once raise the possibility, the concerns, whatever they were, that prompted you to make that phone call. You didn't temper my passion; not raising your hand as in *Hey, let's talk about this*, as in a warning, is just as bad as not telling me why. My dreams are full of floating question marks swimming about like schools of fish: dazzling, but ultimately devoid of answers. You are nothing there.

My bed is cold, unbearably so, even with the heat going full blast. Come melt me with a kiss, the first of many to trigger a tsunami of passion; any excuse, even a lie, will do as long as I see you again, rubbing my face across the contours of your chest, inhaling the residue of sweat and musk embedded in the fur. I am an ice cube waiting in your hand.

Your house is small in reality, but it looms large as a mansion in my dreams.

There, as we come closer to your house, the malls and the chain food restaurants fall away into ever increasing swaths of farmland and forest shucking the cornhusks of suburbia.

There the evergreens huddle together in shades of green and gray.

There the crossroads with a single yellow sign point left and right. The road on the right takes us past a dingy tavern laced with crud-covered neon and a rust-lined gas station half a mile apart.

There another turn on the right: the road sings like a transistor radio from long ago, filled with songs familiar as gloves on your hands.

There by the road is your mailbox post. Painted black with a red flag. I want to be the letter you never thought you would get but did.

There by the house is a gravel driveway and a two-car garage that you've converted into a woodworking workshop. Inside sits a long lathe, an electric bandsaw, and a drill press. Off to the side are all kinds of wood pieces and unfinished pieces of furniture, and on the wall hang a hundred and one hand tools. The promise of stain and varnish awaits them all.

There in the yard are the great woods knotted with low branches and trunks too close to each other.

There through the woods is a path that your cigar-cock knows.

There in the belly of the woods you will find me, waiting for you. Baby, don't you know that I've got your favorite cigar right here? I've got the match right here in my lips. All you have to do is to strike-kiss it with your lips.

Just. Combust.

We'll burn down the woods, the lands, the garage, the house. The smoke will cloud everything until we spasm from orgasm. Around us will be charred remains, but you and I will be untouched and alive and free. We will never turn into ash.

From afar, maybe a half block away, stood a thin gangly man. Bright black curly hair. Slightly petulant lips. He wore a parka, ragged jeans, and Converse sneakers even though it was icy on the sidewalks. I couldn't shake the suspicion that I'd seen him somewhere before. I was waiting for you out in front of Brewe Sisters, and I was too excited to stay inside even though it was starting to snow. I couldn't wait to see you again.

Your blue truck came right up, and I hurried inside. It had been one of those awful weeks at work. It was so bad that I couldn't always concentrate long enough to read my newest Jeanette Winterson novel at night, and I adore her writing!

As you drove us past that man, I saw him give you an unexpected look of bitterness.

"Did you know him?"

You checked the dashboard mirror to see where he was. A flicker of sadness blinked from your eyes.

"Oh, he's just a nut. Don't mind him."

That weekend I kept wondering about him. What had he done to you?

My first hookup after you was horrible. He was one of those NSA-only guys from a hookup app, which suited my pressing need perfectly.

I went over to his apartment, which was about a mile away. His place was messy and reeked of cat although I didn't see the creature, but he didn't seem to care about making a good impression. The minute I stepped into his place, he didn't say anything. He pulled me right into his arms, and we immediately tongued each other. I felt his body. It was a shock to see how much smaller-chested he was. I'd been so used to the bulk of you that I felt thrown off balance, but he held on to me.

When we finally ejaculated, I'd felt an enormous relief, but it wasn't in a good way. I couldn't wait to get the sex over with. He was too pushy, too grunty, too porn-star.

Sex with him made me miss you all the more. That was the exact moment when I realized I wasn't young anymore. I had become officially middle-aged.

Somehow I don't believe you when you say you got right on with the program after you lost your right foot. I don't believe you when you say you didn't cry after learning that they had to amputate the bottom half of your shin. I don't believe that you lay there in your bed, thinking *I'm gonna be a tough man today.* I don't believe you had an Oscar-winning moment of triumph. I don't believe any of that.

Here's what I believe.

You were angry as hell.

You didn't like having to use the walker to get around. You hated having to watch the miserable twig of your shin be rebandaged over and over again, having to wear a shrinker to push the swelling down. You didn't like waiting in your bed and watching the bland soap operas on daytime television. You hated having to learn how to manage your pain and conserve your energy when moving around. You didn't like weighing down on your prosthetic shin-and-foot when trying to walk. Felt too fake, effeminate, contraption-like; it still hurt even after much physical therapy. Maybe you thought about sticking to forearm crutches, but your doctor said that it wouldn't be good for your body long-term. No matter. You'd show how tough, how made of flint you were. Your arms, hands, wrists killed with every gunshot you made with your crutches thumping across the sidewalk, pavement, anywhere. Didn't matter what kind of floor it shot; your foot, sized at 14EEE, was the head of hammer that swung down on the anvil to bounce up the jolt of ball hitting the bell's bottom, the ding that announced to everyone you were different, therefore demanding respect.

I bet you were just an oversized muscular man in his late thirties who screamed and snarled at anyone who came into the room. You hated the tasteless meals on the tray. You spat out curse words at your physical therapist. You did not want to swim in that water for "exercise" or "therapy," because it meant exposing yourself as an amputee. You bawled long after the visiting hours were over. You wondered how you were going to walk again. You thought about how painful it would be to feel the grip of the shin brace holding your prosthetic foot. You hated it all, and you wanted to die.

But something inside you told you to live.

I'm grateful that you listened. You learned to adapt and adopted your prosthetic foot after all.

You are the most beautiful man alive.

You are at your most eloquent when you speak silences. I've listened to you speak in that rarest of tongues, and I've learned that it's not the words that matter but the unstated intent. In that you are a master poet.

I am just babble.

Your eyes sang poetry.

I don't know how you did that, but you did. Each time when I looked up into your eyes, you let loose a sly grin. I couldn't speak your tongue, but I understood it momentarily, a peculiar dialect among men who've had to hide their own feelings. They may sit around and jabber away with beers in their hands, but they do not ever speak it in front of others. That would be too sissy. Once in a while, when they feel as if their souls are dying, they speak poetry and they feel magically restored.

It is indeed hard to know a man on his terms.

He is taught early on to be tough, and if he can't be tough, he can expect a lifetime of teasing. Children cannot fathom a life as adults where they won't be teased, so the scars run deeper than rivers until they turn permanent as marrow.

I couldn't be tough. I knew I was different, but that was all.

You've never mentioned whether you felt different from the others while growing up.

You were a quarterback. Were you interested in guys then?

You told me you hung out in public restrooms, but you never told me what happened your first time. How did you know you liked guys?

Stories like that are important. They tell the story of you.

I thought I'd told you the story of me, but I realized that I never told you anything all that important. I was afraid you'd laugh at me.

The true story of me is filled with embarrassment, humiliation, and shame.

I've never told you how Dad whipped me every time I cried until I learned to cry into the suffocating arms of my pillow.

I've never told you how kids used to call me Fairy Badamore. I was surprised that the nickname hadn't traveled to my family.

I've never told you how I had to escape to the public library with every intention of hiding in there until the day I died. Mr. Loneliness proposed marriage to me, and I accepted. The best part of our marriage were the children he gave me, and they all had names with grand family histories I couldn't get enough of: *Wuthering Heights, Silas Marner, Jane Eyre, Great Expectations,* and *Emma.* I felt intimate with each child, and I felt sad when I had to let each one go. The words on the pages were the same as a best friend whispering into my ear: "You'll be all right."

I long to whisper in your ear: "You are more than all right."

We two wouldn't have to be ghosts anymore.

Disabled people roam everywhere in this city.

Of course, they've always existed, but I'd never paid them much attention. Once you've seen one wheelchair, you've seen them all, right? Same thing with walkers and powered strollers and canes and so on.

But after you hung up on me, I started seeing you everywhere. It was as if your prosthetic foot had transmogrified into something else. I saw you sitting there in a powered scooter going down an aisle in a food co-op. I saw you waiting by the counter with your cane as a salesclerk pulled out a book from the shelves for you. I saw you wearing bicyclist gloves and pushing your wheelchair along from one street corner to another. Then I saw you ambling along with your walker onto the public transit bus I was on. Everyone seemed disgruntled when they had to wait for the driver to flip out the small lift plate in the entrance and hoist you from the curb onto the bus, but I didn't mind. I thought of you, and I just about cried.

But I didn't. I figured that you didn't seem to have cried for me, and therefore I shouldn't cry for you either. I had to be a man just like you.

Those six months when I was with you I had to butch it up. You never asked me to, but I felt I had to. I had seen your masculine friends. I had also seen your small town, and it didn't seem gay-friendly. Yet you were very comfortable where you were, and you said that everyone knew you were gay, but no one talked about it. Sure, everyone talked about their spouses and kids, but not you. *Look what a tough fucker I am*, you seemed to be saying. You were just a beefy tall man with a beard and a machismo attitude. You swaggered a bit even with your crutches.

When I first met you, I was wearing a T-shirt, jeans, and boots. That was the *de rigueur* dress code for bear events. Guys who came wearing shirts that were ironed and who had moisturized their faces were looked down on. They were too faggy; couldn't be bears at all. I felt sorry for some of them. They didn't ask to be skinny or smooth at all, and yet they were accursed with a fetish for a certain body type. Most bears sleep with other bears; they rarely slept with others outside their community. I was grateful for aging in this regard. I was able to gain a bit of weight; not intentionally, of course, but it helped me achieve something of that bearish look. James, would you have been interested in me if I were still skinny?

After I met you, I stopped wearing button shirts on weekends. I simply wore T-shirts and jeans. I wanted to be the kind of bear you'd want. I wasn't sure if you wanted to have me behave like a cub. I was never sure. You never said whether you liked this or that shirt on me. The more I think about it, the more I realize that you'd never complimented me again after our first night.

You said you loved our amazing sex.

You couldn't wait until we could fuck again. You said so on the phone.

But not once in our six months together did you say again that I was cute or handsome or hot.

I told you over and over again what an amazing looker you were.

Anytime when I was impressed by what you'd done with your woodworking, I said so.

And you did have a killer smile!

Maybe you thought I was being charitable because you were disabled. Not really. I know what it feels like not to have your work noticed. Call it the Golden Rule or even good karma, but I've tried to treat you the same way I'd hoped to be treated.

Was I not worth a single compliment?

Please understand that I don't need a lot of praise, but a well-placed compliment could do wonders.

Just call me and tell me how much you've missed me. That would be the greatest compliment you could give me.

To the sacred ground we shall return, ashes to ashes. We shall be absolved of any and all misunderstandings once so rife in the hollow caskets of our hearts, and we shall spread our fierce wings like angels, blessed at last and freed to be fully ourselves without fear, toward the heavens from where we make mad love without shame or hesitation and pray that others after us will learn the difficult lessons far more quickly than we did.

I happened to watch a badly shot clip online of two shaggy-looking men, fully clothed in T-shirts and jeans, wrestling in a mud pit. There weren't a lot of details; it was just so fuzzy with bad sound. It was probably shot on VHS. They rolled and twisted with sudden bouts of humping against each other. I wasn't sure what to make of the spectacle. The more I watched it, the more I envied them. They were absolutely joyous about letting go, not caring what others might think, feeling the taboo sensations of mud pushing up against patches of their skin exposed between their clothes. I couldn't tell if they'd uttered cries of orgasm. There was so much motion in the shimmers of shadow.

A moment later the video cut to the same men standing. They were so covered with mud that you couldn't tell if they were naked at first. They waded into a creek and pulled each other down into the shimmering water. They pushed waves of water over each other and brushed clumps of mud off each other's backs. They burst out laughing, but I couldn't hear what had been so funny. Didn't matter. These two men were bathing together, and they were happy. They had undergone the grunge of passion, and they were rewarding themselves with the baptism of each other.

In that moment, I felt waves of peace wash over me. These men had worshipped each other, gods no doubt in each other's eyes, with holy love and respect in a way that made sense only to them. It was the most spiritual ritual I'd witnessed in a long time.

How I'd sorely missed our Friday night revivals, and how we'd spoken feverishly in incoherent tongues until we both exploded in the same language. No matter where we are, no matter the age we live in, we must seek the spiritual. Even if it's just a ghost. It's better than living without a dream.

Let us go down, you and I, to the big circus not of today but of the yesteryear when cell phones existed only in the most farfetched science fiction of the day. We are still in the age of loud-racketed machine caught in the yawp of clopping horse and carriage. Up ahead is the big awning of blue, the tired wooden poles stretching the burlap skin across the sky, the rickety and paint-peeled train cars locked onto their tracks. We can still smell the manure clumped across the hay-strewn road to the box office, the lurid posters, the blare of promises to see things never seen or heard before: FREAKS. We have come here to see the creatures, the ones who are too short, too tall, too far removed from all we'd thought possible with the human body. The barker, tall and wiry with a Van Dyke that flaps in the wind, exhorts us to come this way, it's only five cents, see the boy with no legs, look at the lady with a full beard, gawk at the pinheaded Cinderella in her sad Miss Havisham dress. You are wearing a tank top and a pair of gym shorts, so there's no mistaking the missing foot as you hop along with your crutches. The music of a calliope tweets notes out of tune. We file past disfigured bodies lit by kerosene, their eyes hidden in shadow as they watch us suppress our gawks. Others near us are silent, grossed out; a few, gasps of horror as these creatures, their faces immobile from years of being laughed at, remain mute. Strange that no one has stared at your missing foot; not even these creatures have shown a flicker of acknowledgment, a possibility of brotherhood with you. You are an amputee; yes, a FREAK. Stranger that no one has noticed my naked body, tattooed with words like FAIRY QUEER FAGGOT COCKSUCKER WRITER; it's as if everyone is seeing right through us. Are we too much for anyone, or are we good enough as fodder in the ongoing war for equality?

Oh, do let us go down, you and I, and join those FREAKS parading before all. They are the brave ones, but let's not be of the audience clapping politely out of discomfort. Let us hold hands, embrace each other with our bulges touching, and tongue each other's mouths like a serpent wrapped around the body of Eve pulling her into itself, swallowing the placenta of tongue deep within her womb into its own alimentary canal consuming the last of her innocence until she turns evil, all-knowing with a what-the-fuck-do-you-want sneer. The smell of sawdust masks the dung of horse and elephant in the distance as the aerialists spin around velvet ropes and twirl between bars swaying to meet, but our spotlighted presence below them will strip everything, their dearly held misconceptions of us whatever they are, that even our rankness will overpower the sickly scent of caramel popcorn. Let them all shriek at how horrifying we are, how dare we offend their sense of propriety, how we are making them sick with showing them the very thoughts that feel absolutely normal to us. Let's give them what they want because they're so afraid to see how abnormal they truly are inside. Why else did they come here? They don't have the strength to look deep inside the funhouse of mirrors deflecting the uglies oozing from the pits of their souls, but we do. We mirror more than they, and they know it. That's why we are more powerful than they'll ever be, damnably so. Why else would they pay to gawk? Pity may be cheap, but compassion is more rare than gold vaulted in the annals of Fort Knox. I call myself a FREAK, though not physically disabled like you, because it's the only way any one of us will ever stop feeling like one. We are all FREAKS inside. I say, FREAK on, baby. Let's FREAK, let's all be FREAKS. Let them gaze their ableist eyes on us and die from the nuclear explosions of our strength. We are da nuke bomb.

Chatting online with disabled guys from all over the country was an eye-opening experience. I had no idea how cruel and denigrating able-bodied men could be toward them. Yet there was no trace of bitterness in the way they shared their stories. Sometimes I cried for them without them knowing it, and I was grateful that I wasn't on webcam. I didn't want to seem like one of those people who got off on inspiration porn or felt sorry for them. They'd simply wanted to be treated as equal to anyone else, especially on dates. I didn't know what to think or feel when a few of them lamented the fact that I had lived so far away. Ah, the curse of the Internet!

I didn't think I was that handsome, but they said I truly was. They gave me their phone numbers and email addresses, but I never contacted any of them outside the gay disability groups online. I was afraid to hear desperation in their voices, and that would've made me feel guilty if I realized someone wasn't for me. Nothing to do with his disability, but . . . let me give you an example. I once talked with this nice-looking fella who had been a wheelchair user since he was seven years old, and he was still living with his parents. He had full use of the upper half of his body, and he was thirty years old! He'd never had a chance to live independently on his own. That prospect scared me a lot more than the reality of his wheels.

I fell into chatting online with a local wheelchair guy named Matt. He was a theater director, which surprised me. Maybe I'm not very bright, but I couldn't honestly imagine a wheelchair user *directing* a show. How would he get around the theater, and onto the stage? I suspected that many theaters in the city had wheel-chair-accessible bathrooms, but it had never occurred to me whether the stage itself was. Matt impressed me with the depth and breadth of his knowledge. He knew so much about theater, and he could rattle off his favorite playwrights like a teenybopper reciting a list of her favorite performers without giving it much thought. I agreed to meet him at Cold & N'ice not too far from my house a few nights later.

When I walked out of my house, I realized that my place wasn't wheelchair-accessible. The front of my house had a number of steps, and . . . oh, crap. There was no way I could casually invite him in for a cuppa coffee and have sex with him. This wasn't going to be a date, I reminded myself; it was just a friendly get-together. The closer I came to the ice cream parlor, the more dread arose in me. I would say some unintentionally wrong thing, and he'd chew me out for not knowing any better. Or I would spot him in a corner and bolt.

But I thought of you. I was meeting him precisely because of you. I wanted to understand your world better. How else could I learn if you weren't around to teach me? I pushed the door open, and I glanced around. I felt a wave of panic when I didn't see Matt anywhere. The place was packed with families and dates licking their cones and chatting away. I thought of leaving right then and there, but I heard the door opening with a grunt. I turned and saw him. He was better-looking than I'd expected. He wore a red t-shirt and a pair of jeans, but I didn't expect to see such wizened fingers packed into his bicyclist gloves.

"Hi, Bill. Sorry that my ride was a bit late, but . . ." he extended his hand, which I shook. "Here we are."

"Nice to meet you in person finally, Matt."

I felt ashamed to be standing so tall like that next to him. I didn't want to be someone who literally looked down on him. I missed looking up to you and rubbing my face across your massive pecs. There was no chance of me doing that with Matt. I'd have to get down on my knees and pretend that he was taller and bigger than me. I'd be acutely aware of the fact that he was in a wheelchair.

As Matt wheeled to the counter and gave his order after I took mine, I looked for an empty table. There was one by the window. I went over there and moved one chair to another table. I watched his eyes as he navigated, quite skillfully might I add, around the haphazardly arranged tables. I felt guilty over the fact that it was easy for me to walk around tables without much thought.

He wheeled himself into place and reached down to lock his brakes.

As he licked his ice cream, I noted his biceps. "You work out?"

"Not really, but this"—he pointed to his wheelchair—"is my gym. Can't avoid working out every day when I go out."

"Well, those muscles look good on you."

"Oh, yeah?" He glanced at his arms. "I figured you'd go for them. Guys who wanna have sex with wheelies are obsessed with my biceps." He winked at me.

I felt a tinge of blush.

"No big worries. I'm glad we met."

"Thank you." I didn't know what else to say. How was it possible that I could talk so easily with a stranger online and feel speechless with him in person?

"To be honest, I rarely meet guys from online. They just focus on my arms or my wheelchair. It's like there's nothing else between my arms and down there and my wheelchair. But you . . . you're different. You're real smart. I like that. Plus the fact that you don't care for Andrew Lloyd Webber."

"Sondheim is just more interesting. I think he's a bit overcomplicated at times, but he does put a lot of thought into what he writes."

"Right, and I still want to do *Into the Woods* one day . . ."

"Yeah, that would be so cool."

"...with disabled performers playing all the characters. I think that would really make some people nervous."

I stopped. "Um."

"Are you upset?"

"I don't know. It's just . . ."

"I'm comfortable with myself. Just like how you're comfortable with being gay."

"But those characters are from classic fairy tales—you can't—they'd look more like freaks!"

"Exactly. Fairy tale characters were always freaks, so why not remind them of this fact? What makes you think that able-bodied actors should always play able-bodied characters? See, that's what we were talking about the other night. Ableist privilege. You assume that because you're able-bodied, you expect the world to be reflected *your* way all the time. You're already upset when I expect to exercise my disability privilege. And you expect me to just take it when you exercise your ableist privilege?"

I felt like crying. "I'm sorry. I didn't mean to—"

"It's no different from how you filter the world through the eyes of a gay man. You see homophobia, and you want to see a world free of ignorance and hate."

He took my hand into his, and I'm sorry to report this, but I recoiled from his touch.

"I can't. This . . ."

"Bill, it's okay. You said you wanted to have your thinking challenged so you could appreciate what it's like to be disabled."

I sighed.

"Why did you want to be challenged? You've never said why."

"I don't know what I was thinking when I said that."

"Was there someone you loved? Was he a cripple?"

I nodded.

"Well, he's not me, and I'm not him. Please get that straight in your head. If you've got issues with him, resolve them with him, not me. I don't need another disability devotee in my life."

"'Disability devotee'? What's that?"

"What does that sound like? An able-bodied person who gets off on inspiration porn and being with a person just because he's disabled. Likes to help out and feel useful. Nothing to do with him as a person at all. The disability, the helplessness, is the star attraction here."

"Oh. I'm sorry. I'd never meant to—"

"I know you didn't. That's why I'd agreed to meet with you."

"How do you know I'm not a . . . that? It sounds so twisted."

"Well, people can be odd sometimes. I know this deaf guy who wore hearing aids, and he said he'd never felt like a freak at all until one day this hearing guy wanted to wear his hearing aids while having sex with him. He wanted to pretend he was deaf."

"Oh, that's so . . ." For a moment I didn't feel like eating my raspberry chocolate ice cream.

"Yeah. But if both people are happy, well—who am I to judge?" He shrugged. "Point is, you're not like that. I could tell from the kind of questions you were asking. It's hard to find someone who's willing to learn what it's like to be disabled. You never suggested how I could do things better. Not once. That speaks volumes about you as a person."

"Well, I've never felt comfortable about telling someone to do something. I mean, I'd have assumed that he's tried all the options."

"Exactly. Now may I hold your hand?"

"Uh, why?"

"Because I want to feel good about holding a sexy guy's hand. You're hot stuff. You do know that, right?"

I didn't know what to say or do. I was scared. I was afraid of being seen in public like that. No, no—scratch that. I didn't feel comfortable with a wheelchair user holding my hand. I knew I wasn't going to pick up some contagion from him, but I feared that my acceptability factor within the able-bodied community would drop quite a few notches if they saw me holding a disabled man's hand. You were different. You were tall and beefy as any ex-quarterback would be, and you could stand up to your full height. No one would know about you as long as you wore pants and socks. But Matt? His height sitting up was nowhere near your magnificent height that spoke of sturdy birch trees. He was just a shrub.

I know I'm being unfair to Matt. I'd never realized how shallow and mean I could be until that night I met him. The sickening truth is that if Matt wasn't in a wheelchair, I wouldn't have minded him holding my hand. Does that make me an asshole? I think it does. Should I have asked to sleep with him that night? I was afraid that he'd say he didn't want to be a pity fuck.

But I didn't bolt. I didn't want to hurt his feelings.

"For someone who talks a lot online, you're awfully quiet."

"I'm sorry. I'm just not ready for this." I withdrew my hand. "I mean, you're a nice guy and all, but . . ."

"I came on too strong, did I?"

"I think so. Yeah."

"I thought this was supposed to be a date."

"I don't know."

"Look, Bill. Look at me."

I looked into his deep blue eyes. Funny how I'd never noticed them before. I must've been too focused on his wheels.

"I thought you were smart enough to get me. I'm just like any other guy out there. I'm . . . you know, lonely sometimes and, well . . ."

"It's okay. Maybe this was a mistake."

"You're still thinking of him."

"What are you talking about?"

"Him. The first disabled guy in your life. Whoever he is."

"How do you know he was my first?"

"Because you're not comfortable with me as I am."

"That's not true."

"You prefer the fantasy of his disability."

"You don't know anything about my situation."

"I don't have to. Able-bodied guys are the same way. They meet someone special who happens to be disabled, and they break up, and then they want to meet someone else disabled because they're still in love with him. I'm here to tell you that if you date someone like me because of my wheels, you're not being fair to me. I'm my own person, and I'm not just my wheels. Got that?"

I'd never felt so small. I felt so ashamed that I wanted to turn into a cockroach and have him roll over me. I didn't realize I was crying until I tried to speak. "I'm sorry." My voice was a hoarse whisper. "I wasn't thinking . . ."

I was surprised when he took my hand again.

"What—what are you doing?"

"You're not scaring me away. I'm still interested in you."

A long moment of sniffling came and went. I blew my nose into a napkin. "Sorry."

"It's cool." He resumed licking his ice cream cone. "What films have you watched lately?"

We talked until the place closed, but I couldn't go to bed with him. Just couldn't.

Yes, I know. I'm very shallow.

We exchanged phone numbers, but he never called me back. His number's taped there on that wall above my desk. Sometimes it haunts my dreaming.

When you and I caught up on our week in the car toward your house on those Friday evenings, you turned on the radio. They were full of country songs about love gone wrong, made so right, and never regained. I never cared for country music until after you hung up. Sure, there were a number of country singers I'd found sexy, but then I discovered Drake Jensen. I couldn't believe that a man like him could be so open about being gay, and with a good voice blessed with a hint of gravelly growl. That was a revelation. Suddenly his music wasn't full of songs about loving a woman. I loved in one music video how honest he was about trying to find a special guy online through Bear411, and how expressive he was with his face. It was so easy to read his face because his emotions were an open book. He was so comfortable with himself no matter how he'd performed that it was easy to fall for him. There in his sleeveless flannel shirt and boots on the railroad tracks and cargo shorts on the beach, he reminded me of the you I'd longed to see once you'd stopped dying. He was fully alive, flesh and blood, with his sexy voice and his furry tattooed body, and he wasn't afraid to display so much of himself on camera. I knew he gained that powerful strength and confidence from the man he so loved. I wanted to be that man to give you the same pride in being different.

I thought I was strong enough to love you as you were, but you must've seen me as too weak for the yoke of your fearful heart. I tell you, no matter how young you might've seen me as, I would've been strong as an ox. Remember, I'm a farmer's son. I'd have surprised you with my inner strength. I would've plowed the fields of sorrow until your garden was blooming with sunflowers heavy with the sweetest seeds yet to be plucked by crows. I would've freed you from the needless prison of that fear of being seen as weak because you needed to be sentimental now and then, just like those sappy films of the 1930s with their predictable happy endings. You wouldn't feel embarrassed about pulling some daisies from the backyard and giving them to me with a kiss. You wouldn't be afraid to crack a smile if I made a goofy joke at your expense. And you'd feel strong enough to hold my hand in public no matter where we were, just like Drake was with his husband striding out of a tall building out onto a beach in my favorite video of his. You'd nod your head at me before we kissed against the backdrop of the sunset.

I'd be your favorite country song.

My memories are mottled like trees of different heights and shapes. You'd think that being trees, they're pretty much similar, but the aura of memory is a dense fog lost in the woods. It's hard to see sometimes when I travel toward an odd sound, a partially erased face, a conversation lined with gaps, and when I trip over a tree's root tentacle, I find myself waking up to something else I'd not realized had been there all along.

Like: you once mentioned your father was a schoolteacher at your high school. You never said what your mother did for a living. Probably a housewife. You never said whether you had brothers and sisters.

Like: your favorite vegetable was rutabaga. You didn't care all that much for fancy food.

Like: you'd grown up two hours northwest of my hometown where winters were long as hell; summers, fleetingly short like fireflies.

Like: you didn't like having liquor around the house.

Like: you were a big hockey fan. You wanted to play in high school, but you were too tall and gawky on the ice.

Like: you mentioned that you played quarterback for your high school. I didn't tell you this, but I did look through your high school yearbooks once when you were taking a shower. It was surreal to see you look so young and quite thin, but your height was obvious. You had posed with your hand on the ball, and you kept one arm behind your back. Those thighs were already mighty. You looked tough and menacing even though you were clean-shaven. There was no way anyone would fuck with you. I tried to imagine you, a rising star on the football field, torn between seeing your dad at school and wanting to be one of the cool jocks.

Like: in your living room I saw the framed picture of your daughter, Annie, perched atop the mantelpiece above the fireplace. It looked like it had been taken in the mid eighties. You had more hair, and you sported only a mustache. You still looked hot. She wore a cute striped jumper, and she was probably five years old. Her head was at your waist, and she was looking brightly into the sun of you. Her eyes squinted, but there was no mistaking that winsome smile of hers.

You caught me looking at the picture.

A shadow crossed your face.

The following weekend it was gone from the mantelpiece.

It had been a crack in your façade.

I thought about the absence of that picture a great deal long after I'd seen you last.

I am a wisp.

I am not one of those spectacular beauties who will win a popularity contest.

I am a figment of smoke that once curled upward from the end of your cigar.

I am a moan, a grunt, a cry, a yell, a contented sigh.

I am a tiny fire constantly shielded from your eyes.

The wick of my heart is burning down to an ashen nub.

With summer wearing down, I find myself starting to forget the particulars of your body. It's as if each of my memories has been retouched with a slight fuzzy blur. Just how huge were your nipples? How thick, how long was your cock? Were your shoulders truly covered with the thickest fur I'd ever touched? All that has started to fade, but I will never forget the size and bulk of you as you hovered over me and stared into my eyes when we pumped away. You rarely gazed at me so directly, and for so long.

Time was always put on hold when we forgot about everything but our bodies reaching out to each other. It was so easy to lose track of time when we rollercoastered up and down with the tempos of our lovemaking. We were always shocked by the time on your bedside clock. I wanted more of that with you, not noticing how quickly our years together were passing by.

All I got from you was a winter of memory and too many seasons of ache.

When I noticed that Valentine's Day fell on a Friday, I stopped. Should I get you a card, or would it be too much, too soon? I went to We Are Family, a T-shirt and trinket shop littered with rainbow-flavored flags, underwear, and key rings; probably the last of its kind that's not overlooking a gay beach. There were racks of naughty valentines, usually revealing a naked man with an impossibly large endowment on the inside. Somehow, as alluring and attractive these men were, none felt right. I decided to try the funny cards. A few did make me laugh, but none struck me as suitable for you.

When I put another card away in exasperation, I happened to look up. The man with the curly hair—you'd called him a "nut"—was in the other end of the store; he was browsing a pile of deeply discounted erotica titles. With his parka and stone-washed jeans, he looked the same as before. Closer, and without feeling that he could catch me looking at him, I observed that he had some gray in his hair. I'd initially pegged him to be in his forties, but I realized that he had to be closer to your age. The slenderness was what had thrown off my estimation of his age. I couldn't tell if he knew I was there, or if he had simply lost interest in me.

I picked up another card. It was most unfunny; cheesy and tacky. Then it occurred to me that a perfect valentine card would have a still of Carole Lombard in a silly pose and a pithy quote of hers from one of her movies. Of course, there wasn't any such thing, not even of *any* glamorous starlet from the Golden Age of Hollywood. I was feeling at a loss when I happened to look up again.

The curly-haired stranger, standing by the door about to pull it open, gave me the queerest smile; as if he knew who I was, or had known a secret I didn't know I had. He turned and left. Why did he smile like that?

I ended up not giving you a card or wishing you a Happy Valentine's Day. Yet, on that night you were quite randy. Almost too much: you kissed me very hard, fucked me very hard, sucked me very hard. I wanted to tell you that you didn't have to try so hard, but I didn't want to kill the mood. You were such a stud that you didn't need to act like a porn star at all to get me going. Still, your passion was all the valentine I needed.

I try to remember the last time we had sex.

That Sunday morning we had just awakened, and you were horny. I knew exactly what you wanted. I lifted my legs, and you lubed up for entry.

Once inside, I'd never seen you sweat so much. You were thrusting so hard, it almost hurt. There was something different in your face; as if you had become possessed by a different persona, but it was still recognizably you.

You looked so relieved when it was over.

I was too, but I felt scared. I couldn't figure out why, but the fear of losing you flashed through me. "You okay?"

"Yeah."

"You sure?"

"Yeah. Just a lot of things on my mind."

That surprised me. We had been together all that weekend, and this was the first time you'd mentioned a potential problem of any kind. "What things?"

"Oh, just . . ." You waved me away with your hand.

"You can tell me."

"It's not worth it."

"Do you trust me?"

"It's not that, dammit." You pushed yourself off the bed and hopped to the bathroom door. "I should go shower now."

While I lay between your flannel sheets and listened to the water hiss all over your body, I wanted to hold your hands and let you feel the love shimmering up my spine and down my arms and hands right into yours.

When you came out of the shower and pulled on your clothes, I smiled.

You gave me a tight smile, as if you weren't sure whether you should be happy. Then it was back to the same old face of yours. Nothing happened, and yet everything did.

I have always liked winter. Always. The whiteness, the grayness, the blackness—the world turns monochromatic for a long moment. An assiduous chill burrows into my marrows, and I feel dead in the most alive way possible. I boil with the ache to stay warm, but all this will be temporary. The seasons will change again and again, and winter is just a season. I love winter the most because I'm the least loved in my family and it's the least loved time of year. The days hurry by as if they couldn't wait to get home, and in each long darkness I breathe entire books in the candlelight of my dreams. Here, I'm a writer learning to read, and a reader learning to write. The words I consume will kindle the fire deep in my bones, and soon I will be feverish with characters and stories I didn't know existed. I don't feel like an orphan anymore.

But no one warned me that if a man leaves you in the dead of winter, he puts you at risk of hypothermia. Naked, you will drown in a sea of snow and sorrow.

There were nights when I shivered incessantly in my flannel sheets. My teeth wouldn't stop chattering. I wanted that annoying sound to stop. I wanted to take a leather belt and wrap it around my jaw and strap its buckle atop my head so I could sleep in peace. My teeth kept hitting, tapping out the Morse code of your name nonstop. I wanted to be warm enough so my tears wouldn't freeze in midstream down my face.

The day you hung up on me was the first day of spring. My memories of those days that followed were gray with the full thrust of winter even when the winds turned balmy and the snow melted into the richest greens everywhere. It didn't matter that I could walk outside with only a T-shirt and shorts; I still felt cold from the icy absence of you. I was feverish with dreams of you that didn't make sense enough to create a narrative of any kind. I was a bad experimental film from the sixties. Everyone talked about the glorious weather, but my heart was still a hopeless rusty weathervane that kept swinging back north to your house.

Then came the Pride Festival that June.

I thought of you all that weekend. I wondered if you'd come down to the festival and scan the sea of men for your next victim. You'd mastered the art of emotional unavailability to the point that everyone had thought you were indeed ready to date. Maybe I should be more like you, aiming for a permanent flint-like expression like Clint Eastwood's, looking unavailable and therefore hotter. You've figured this out. I know you have. There's something potent about a man of mystery, and he demands to be solved. He says he's not ready for a relationship, but he doesn't push away the sexual advances. He wants to cheat on Mr. Loneliness too, except that in his case, divorcing him would be emotionally expensive in court. He will forever doubt whether he's made the right decision, and when he's decided that he has, he may find that the other man has already moved on. The other man will rightly feel that he was never loved.

Like me.

Some nights, after we had sex, you turned on the TV in the bedroom. I watched you open the humidor. It was as if you were a rabbi opening up the Torah. You took a cigar out, and you held it up to the lamp after unwrapping its cellophane. You stroked it a bit and sniffed the promise of its aroma. You were meticulous about preparing a cigar; you had to snip the glued end just so. Then you struck a match and lit up your piece.

How it caught a gentle but fierce fire when you breathed in, and how I longed to be that cigar, to be the center of so much devotion. Draw my soul deep into the cavern of your mouth, and remember just how I taste. I'm the richest-flavored smoke you can ever hope to find.

Each time I inhaled the darkest crevices of your body, I thought of the potting soil I used for my plants. How deep and rich it was to smell the essence of root and mineral. How hungry it was for water and chlorophyll. How pungent it was to live. You planted seeds each time you burrowed deep into me. It was as if I grew another inch. I wasn't a sapling anymore. I was a tree. You had turned me into something I never thought I was capable of being: a tree. The thin film of sweat was thick as soil under the grass blades of your fur. How I loved mowing your grassy fur clean. How much I'd learned to imprint the body of you onto the atlas of my tongue. How much I couldn't get enough of you.

That I'll never know how much I'd mattered to you is what's killing me.

I am a tree eaten alive by the elm bark beetle.

I am hollow.

Not even the squirrels want to stash their acorns inside me. It's a matter of time before I'm chopped down and carted away.

I'll become a stump, and my sawn and splintered face will never reveal the number of years lived.

I branch outward every night in my dreams. When my roots are finally pulled out of the ground, my nails will still linger in the soil of you. It will scratch a bit longer for that smell of you filling that gasp of air inside my nails. My memories will turn into gray crescents of moon, and my roots will bristle white.

Have I been loved by something strange, and has it already forgotten me?

A SHADOW FLUTTERY
AMONG THE BIRCHES

What kills love? Only this: Neglect. Not to see you when you stand before me. Not to think of you in the little things. Not to make the road wide for you, the table spread for you. To choose you out of habit not desire, to pass the flower seller without a thought. To leave the dishes unwashed, the bed unmade, to ignore you in the mornings, make use of you at night. To crave another while pecking your cheek. To say your name without hearing it, to assume it is mine to call.

—Jeanette Winterson

At dawn an unexpected fog had descended on the streets where I walked from my house to work. The city wasn't near a major lake, which made the fog stupendous. The mist of gray muffled the sounds of people walking, cars inching with their headlights on. As I walked, I realized I should've brought along a flashlight. Everything, including the cracks of my sidewalk, didn't feel familiar. I was lost in a foreign country right on my own street. The chill permeated my bones. I was a sleepwalker. As much as it felt like a dream, it wasn't. I'd shaven my neck, showered, eaten a banana with a bit of yogurt, and put on fresh clothes.

As I headed closer to Broadway and Hancock, a figure in black strode toward me. The sound of its feet had a slow rhythm, but there was no hesitation, no off-beat from the way it moved. The figure approaching me turned out to be a woman wearing a tight-fitting hat, a black cape, and high-heeled black shoes. She caught sight of my face, and she smiled as if she knew me, as if we'd already met a long time ago. I almost expected her to say my name, but she stopped right in front of me. I was struck by how tall she was; she must have been six feet tall. She spoke sharply, her cadences ringing: "I'm not fluent in French, but I speak the language of night very well."

It was then I knew who she was.

My housemates, Chloë and Veena, have been together for twenty-two years.

When I first met Chloë Nurnberg in our class, Women's Literature from the Nineteenth Century, her skirts struck me. She did not like T-shirts or pants. She was quite schoolmarmish even back then, and her pearl earrings and black glasses were caricatured in chalk on the blackboard behind her desk when she stepped out for longer than a minute to talk with the principal. She was wide-hipped, the reason why she preferred skirts, and she, already an old lady in her mid-forties, wore knitted sweaters over her white blouses. She was the master of the cutting glance that silenced her students. She didn't accept excuses easily; she was not popular. But those who really wanted to learn adored her. She spotted early on those who wanted to learn and gave them subtle nudges when no one was looking so they'd know they were not ignored when a student complained that it was too much work. Every year the new students stayed the same age, and she saw more and more the effects of the mobile technology on them. They were more interested in texting and emailing even during class. One morning she hit on a simple solution. She wrote their last names sideways along the bottom of her blackboard, drawing a line upward between each name, and told the students that if they wanted to graduate from middle school, they had to put their cell phones along the shelf. No one could miss their phones, and when a text message went off, Ms. Nurnberg went to the phone and turned it off. She became proficient in knowing how to shut off a wide variety of phones and insisting that the phones be faced against the wall. It was not long before other teachers adopted her solution. She had grown up with blue-collar parents in a small town in Nebraska, two states away, and they had insisted that she finish high school because they hadn't; she had to go to college for their sake. She didn't know what extraordinary parents they had been until they showed up for her graduation. They had driven all day, taking turns in their small rusted car, and even though they were still tired from sleeping in a strange bed in a cheap motel just out of town, they stood proudly in their Sunday best. Didn't matter that their clothes were cheap-looking compared to what the other parents wore. She didn't care about that because in that moment, after having apprenticed that spring semester and met parents of her students, she realized her own parents were indeed great. They never treated her badly; they expected her to do her chores. They knew the importance of education, and they had pushed her this far. It was because of them she went to graduate school for a master's in teaching. When she told them she was a lesbian, they were disappointed, but not for long. They'd figured that she was a smart lady, and who were they to know what was best for her? She was exceedingly practical, compassionate, and bookish, all of which had endeared her wife, Veena Pelle, to her.

Veena, when she met Chloë at the university, was an unfocused art history student. She tried to do studio art, but she didn't master techniques well enough to bolster her crashing GPA. She had long frizzy hair, a peppering of freckles on her high cheekbones, and white teeth that seemed to light up when she smiled. She had tiny breasts, and she hated her chest flatness so she walked around in sweatshirts, sweatpants, and flip-flops when it was warm out. She didn't care about looking pretty for anyone. She had spent long days alone poring through one book of art reproductions after another at her grandma's house when her parents traveled all over Europe. She tried to draw, she took individual tutoring classes; she knew she wasn't very good, but what else could she do? She loved art, that was all she knew, so she tried again in high school to draw, made collages out of expensive *Artforum* magazines, that sorta thing, but nothing; she knew she wasn't good at anything related to art. She liked walking idly among one painting after another in the museum downtown, and absorbed gorgeously composed black-and-white photographs that seemed to shimmer in the pools of light focused on them. She brought along her sketch-book and tried to copy a Georgia O'Keeffe painting, but she got the charcoaled shading wrong. She wanted art, but she was not an artist, and not into research, but maybe she could teach art history even though those jobs were impossible to find. Her parents told her that it didn't matter, she should just learn what she wanted to learn, and life itself would take care of her. She hated feeling like a failure, so she never told anyone how wealthy her parents were. She didn't want to be seen as a trust fund baby, a dilettante rather than someone seriously committed to something. She was always vague about which neighborhood she grew up in, and she was relieved that none of her friends from the boarding school she attended had come to her university. They were all into the Ivy League thing, but unlike her parents, she didn't like to travel all that much. She thought of dropping out of college, but on that first day of class in the Classics of Modernist Literature, she took the first available seat. Chloë happened to be sitting next to her.

They didn't pay much attention to each other for the first fif-teen minutes until Professor Jane Sharer, after explaining how she'd tabulate their grades, said that they were going to plunge right in. She held up a copy of *Nightwood*, a novel by Djuna Barnes that had been published in 1936 with no less than T. S. Eliot's help, and said, "I'm going to paraphrase something from this book: I have come to tell you of the night." She had been a trained actress before becoming a teacher, so she chose her texts on the basis of whether they had an *ear* for language; not just their historical importance. She enthralled her students with her rendi-tions, sharpening their ears for the nuances of language.

Twenty-two years later, Chloë and Veena still talk about Pro-fessor Sharer, the woman who brought them together. It was Chloë's idea that Veena look into graphic design. Bingo. She has been working at the headquarters of Brewe Sisters Corporation downtown ever since. She's really good at what she does. She often designs amazing posters for her favorite local bands in exchange for their autographed CDs.

In their living room is a much-thumbed copy of *Nightwood*. Most people have never heard of it. It's a slightly trippy novel, a *roman à clef*, actually, in which two women connect in Paris, only to have one of them stolen away by a socialite woman for America. There is a man who has delusions of being of royal blood, and there is a doctor of questionable background. Between them, Paris in the 1920s breathes out what night can only do, seducing everyone in ways most unexpected. The plot may not sound all that significant, but its style of writing is. The dialogue is unrealistic yet compelling; it is a voice utterly like any other. You read it, and you *listen*. You just do.

Chloë and Veena liked to read random passages from the book out loud when they got bored with whatever was on TV. It is still startling to hear a familiar voice speak differently in a voice from the past: ". . . put those thousand eyes into one eye and you would have the night combed with the great blind searchlight of the heart." Whoa. Really stops you, doesn't it? What does it mean? A bit of shadow is all you need to get something lodged permanently in your brain, and no amount of sunlight can get it out. We were conceived in shadow, and therefore hunger for shadow we do even though we know better to look for sunlight. Such are thoughts that trickle into my brain long after I've heard passages from *Nightwood* read out loud.

Of course, they never mention her last name in conversation. Just Djuna. She was the dream love child of every literate lesbian, and she was quite a black cat with a seductive and witty tongue. They read everything of hers, but *Nightwood* was the bible they returned to over and over again. You should've seen their faces when I'd scoured online for a battered copy of the first British edition of *Nightwood*, with its tattered purple and gray cover one Christmas. They squealed with delight. They couldn't stop hugging me all day long. Sometimes they call me Felix when I come home from a lousy date. Or Guido when I'm being too childish. Or Dr. O'Connor when I'm too show-offy with my book smarts. Fans of the novel would know whom I mean.

When they got married twelve years ago, they flew to New York City so they could visit Djuna's last residence on Patchin Place and pay their respects in front of her house by reading out loud their favorite parts of the dialogue between Nora and the doctor from *Nightwood*: ". . . I have come to ask you to tell me everything you know about the night . . ." That was their first Djuna pilgrimage. For the next twelve years, they had been planning their first week in Paris to haunt where she used to live and eat. They left the day after you hung up, and I didn't have the heart to spoil their jubilant anticipation. Being left alone in their house was perfect timing.

When Chloë asked me to move in with them at their house on Houghton Avenue, I'd read the novel once for class and thought the story strange and not quite there. I'd never taken classes under Professor Sharer; her classes were always waitlisted. But after I moved into their big house, their constant allusions and references to the book required that I read the book again. It was difficult to reread it a second time, but I *got* it on my third round. I just fell in awe of Djuna's achievement. Just how did she pull off such an alchemy of seduction and mystery in such stylistically unconventional and yet formal prose? It's very ghostlike. It *is* the language of ghosthood. Echoes are everywhere. It is a book of dark undercurrents that slither deeper than the Seine.

With you, I find myself flailing in the language of haunting. I am forever lost in a city of wet cobblestones and gaslights yearning to pierce the night, the skin of heart. I'm still here, with this Ouija board, waiting for a nudge from you on my planchette.

Do you whisper to yourself in the middle of the night when you think no one is listening? I do.

The music of silences is a symphony on your tongue. Sing to me.

One night when I returned from the bathroom, I found you lying on your back with your hands behind your head. "Come and get me," you said.

With each roam of my hands all over the globe of your belly, I created new maps of desire. I was still a new student of your cartography. It wasn't lust anymore. The hot iron of lust had simmered, but the flame of coals persisted. I still jacked off over you during the week. I never knew where I was going each time I had sex with you. Each time I rubbed my face across the fur of your belly, I felt renewed. I knew my place in the universe, and it was there with you. You were my sun and my moon, and I was a comet returning time and again.

I never thought of you as worthy of poetry. You said you weren't a reader, so I never tried to write anything in your honor. Not even a poem. But each day and night when I have those dream conversations with you, I feel more and more like a poet, kicking and yet helpless. I am seeing things I had never seen before.

What was the point of writing a poem if you'd never cared to read?

If I write a poem, it would be to the stars, the nebulae, the galaxies. They had already lived a thousand and one poems, and they did not need to read anyone's mawkish attempts. They were already masters. That was why they were given a venerated place in the sky.

My sky is so vast and so unpopulated with few stars. Come twinkle, twinkle.

Djuna of the moon, did you forget to dream? You sat in bed and wrote longhand in the comfort of Peggy Guggenheim's rented Hayford Hall the eeriness of losing Thelma first to drink, and then to that chattering socialite. You wanted her again, but she sailed off to New York with that bitch. She left you, there in the city where she lived with you for eight years, in Paris where the literati and glitterati flitted in and out the sad and happy cafés on the Left Bank. The black cloud of anti-Semitism rising from the east had started to cast a long cape of black; the ominous night of glass windows shattering, the rounding up of Jews and other undesirables, was yet to come.

Djuna of the sun, did you forget to forgive? You dipped your pen in the most acid ink of all. You wrote to avenge the very people who'd hurt you. The polygamist father, a man of many talents and languages but cursed with a talent for never being focused long enough to succeed except at breeding more babies. The rape in your teens, even with your father's consent. The anger at having to take care of so many children not yours, and the pit-stomach knowledge that you'd never have children. The deep relief in having your one baby aborted, and the slick sickness of using your abortionist Daniel A. Mahoney—who was certainly no physician—as your doctor character in your little tome. What a microphone ear you'd kept to the page! Oh yes, you would aim your poison arrow at Thelma Ellen Wood and Henrietta McCrea Metcalf, the wealthy woman whom you satirized with the novel's Jenny Petherbridge for collecting people the way she collected things. Their hearts would pump toxins once everyone figured out who Robin and Jenny were. You would outlive them all, and you did.

Djuna of the drink, did you recall the cornhusk of her body when you imbibed another round of liquor? How many bodies had you touched before you met her? The sound of her laughter must've struck you like lovebirds twittering together. The days together were woven intricately like trapeze artists spinning and sailing past each other for another relapse on the swing before another twist and turn of bravura. You tossed the baton of your pen up in the air and spun it so many times that no one could believe what they'd read of you. Mystery with a bit of glitter, laced from revenge, has enshrouded your visage. You are the soprano who sings of nights long gone from Paris, in the days when the dollar was strong and the franc very weak, in the days when Gertrude

Stein held the upper hand on who was hot and who was not, in the days when you didn't know what you had until you lost her.

One Halloween my housemates and I wore the strangest costumes, inspired by *Nightwood*, to a party of mostly literary friends. Chloë dressed up as Nora Flood; Veena, Robin Vote; and I, Matthew O'Connor. Veena did a lot of research into what women would've worn in Paris during the 1920s. In the novel, Nora had caught Matthew wearing a dress late at night so it made sense that I'd have to wear a flannel nightgown.

Chloë and Veena had read somewhere that when Djuna and Thelma were together, they made a striking impression by hooking each other's elbows while wearing capes. Chloë and Veena looked incredible together. We didn't take a lot of pictures, but the ones we did turned out great. They had one of them blown up and hung above Veena's desk.

It was very cold out there, so I bundled up underneath my nightgown. I wore a bad wig. My housemates thought I looked just like the doctor in drag. I got a lot of gasps and guffaws when I walked about, and many people thought I was the mother from Alfred Hitchcock's *Psycho*. I had to explain who I was, and most people gave me blank looks when I mentioned *Nightwood*. After a while, I gave up on explaining and said that I had a hormone problem. Everyone chuckled nervously.

The ladies were of course a hit, but nobody understood who their characters were. All they thought was that they were lipstick lesbians from the 1920s.

The wittiest thing I'd said all night? "Lord, you make me feel like an invert." Only Chloë and Veena broke out laughing.

I couldn't believe that no one there knew what "invert" meant! I was shocked.

Still, it was great fun. Chloë and Veena are the closest thing I have to a family in this city.

I was thinking about this the other day because you and I have never celebrated a holiday together. Was this by design, just to make it clear that we weren't a couple?

Djuna learned her craft as a writer from listening to her grandmother who had done a lot of writing on her own, and from writing the interviews she'd done with noteworthy people around New York City. At one point, she made $7,000 a year, a considerable salary considering that new houses were going for a lot less than that in those days. Her first novel, *Ryder*, was a mishmash of poetry, dreams, fiction, songs, *belles-lettres*, and parables; it was quite autobiographical in depicting her own childhood with a father who not only lived with his wife but also with his mistress. It was all with his mother's beaming approval, and therefore scandalous. She wrote whatever she could to make money, and her specialty was "stunt stories." She became quite famous for a *New York World Magazine* piece called "How It Feels to be Forcibly Fed." A lot of British suffragists had died that way in prison, so she decided to do the same thing in order to convey what it was like. Photographs of her being force-fed through one of her nostrils were published.

But when *McCall's* asked her to write a travel piece about Paris, she agreed and set sail for Paris in 1921. Her first three weeks in Paris filled her with great trepidation until she began meeting other Americans there. Yet that trip changed her life overnight, and as one might say in the annals of queer lit, the rest is her story.

I never thought of you as grotesque. Yes, different, at first, but never grotesque.

Would you think me odd if I said that your missing foot was the most beautiful thing about you? That it meant you weren't a god, and that you were indeed mortal like the rest of us? If you had an impenetrable veneer, you now had a crack, an Achilles heel.

You are the smoke that's never left my tongue.

You're embedded deep in my taste buds. If I think about what you taste like, it's gone. But if I don't think about it, there you are in full flower. You are sweeter than incense.

When I dream of you, my tongue returns to the Garden of Eden.

James, the crow's feet around your eyes are beautiful. The threads of white and gray in the carpet of black fur on your chest are stunning. The creep of fat just under your arms makes your build more imposing. Am I weird in wanting you just as you are?

Society has a way of making anyone feel grotesque about wanting someone they feel should be considered undesirable or in need of repair. I want the you, as you are, before anyone retouches you.

In 1915, Djuna wrote a chapbook of eight poems and five drawings called *The Book of Repulsive Women*. They revealed ambivalent feelings about women's bodies and sexuality, and in later years, Djuna never mentioned the book; disowned it. Too much of an embarrassment, and yet, because she hadn't registered its copyright, the book was reprinted often without her consent. Then came *Ladies Almanack*, in which she filled its lines with inside jokes and literary obscurities that only friends of Djuna's inner lesbian circle with Natalie Clifford Barney would appreciate; she drew images in the style of Elizabethan woodcuts. Critics in later years would argue over it. Was it a satire? An attack?

Then came the first breakup with Thelma Wood in 1927; in that limbo state of mind, Djuna began writing what later became *Nightwood*. Its title went through a few iterations, most notably *Bow Down* and *The Anatomy of Night*. But in the year before it was published, Djuna hit upon its most fitting title, "like night-shade, poison and night and forest, and tough, in the meaty sense." It was not long until, in a letter to a friend, Djuna was struck by the title in a different way: "Nigh T. Wood—low, thought of it the other day. Very odd." Then Thelma and Djuna got back together, but when Thelma met Henrietta McCrea Metcalf in 1928 and left for

America to be with her not long after, Djuna felt as if she'd died. She went on to date a few men, most notably Charles Henri Ford, a bisexual writer who'd twice proposed marriage to her. But when she realized she would not ever again have a love as great as the one she had with Thelma, she became a ghost fighting to stay alive. She had nothing but art to live for.

The tenor that echoes from the mouth of Dr. Matthew O'Connor is rich and Wagnerian; it seems improbable that anyone could talk the way he does, but Djuna did sit down and took notes when Dan Mahoney, her future abortionist, carried on about this and that. He was a short man, a former dancer and boxer, and full of brilliant wit and opinions when he told story after story, riddled with asides, in dimly-lit bars and cafés. She listened, remembered, and embellished his eloquence, but apparently not too much. He was such a force of loquacious nature as Dr. O'Connor, possibly the most distinctive character in *Nightwood*, that he threatened to capsize the novel. No matter how she tried to scale him back, tone him down, his presence haunted every other page even when he wasn't in the room. Dan Mahoney was not easily forgotten; apparently easily recognizable in the book to all who'd met him. According to Charles Henri Ford, he once asked Dan Mahoney what he thought night was after learning that Djuna was writing a chapter about him and the night, and he simply said, "The night is when you realize that you're all wet."

I envy anyone who's had the gumption to live, disappear into the lives of others, only to return not only war-scarred but also wiser with stories only they can tell in their own inimitable voices. Good stories are worth far more than their weight in gold, and those wandering storytellers, especially those disciplined enough to set forth their tales in print, are the true millionaires of any age. I am but a pauper.

After writing *Nightwood*, Djuna tried to write another book for years. Couldn't. She tried to love again and again; it never worked out. Finally, she stopped. Her deepening affair with alcoholism was much easier; at least she could taste something sluicing down her throat and deaden her heart at the same time. She became fanatically private when more and more people, having read *Nightwood* over the years, began showing up at her door in Greenwich Village. Who was the creature who'd written such a mysterious book? A few professed love, and she resisted offers to anthologize her work in lesbian anthologies. The editors of such collections did not understand that she never made the distinction between men and women when she loved: "I'm not a lesbian; I just loved Thelma."

Thelma made her feel alive in their eight years together, but Thelma leaving her quite abruptly made her immortal.

Open a page anywhere in *Nightwood* and a ghost will slip out and haunt you without you quite comprehending why. The language of shadow and memory is full of mystery and ache, all rapt and ripe for translators lost without their dictionaries.

With each technological advance online and with our mobile phones, we find ourselves dissociating more and more from each other. We have turned each other into blips on the screen. We say hello to each other online, and we forget what the other looks like in breathing form. We are scarcely there in person when we greet each other on the street. We've become too comfortable with feeling what we must in front of the computer screen that in the face of another, we suddenly feel the need for masks. We want to run and hide; no wall of text to shield us from their unchecked reactions to our living selves. We watch porn online and let it narrow our sexual thinking into boxes. Our lives have turned into bits and bytes that we have become ghosts even to ourselves. How did we get so haunted?

Our hearts are full of unsolved mysteries. We read in the dark because the ache for definitive answers to our whys haunts us. We are pages of ashes to ashes.

Djuna lived in a time when you couldn't always get a copy of anything easily. If she saw a movie that she liked, she couldn't expect to own a copy of the print one day unless she had her own film projector and the means to buy the print. She had to count otherwise on revival theaters. If she heard a song on the radio, there was no guarantee that she could find the song in the nearest record store. Nothing was instantly downloadable. They had to make do with memory.

Magic and memory go together like bread and butter. Maybe it's better not to know someone too well.

Nightwood reeks of that elusiveness of memory. Everyone wants Robin, but she doesn't understand quite why she keeps leaving someone for another, or what should be the source of her happiness, her unhappiness too. Was it only sex or the want of something more real? Was I not real enough for you?

Sometimes I dream of being lost in Paris of the 1920s late at night. Your name is almost a whisper on my lips, but I don't dare utter it out loud. The winds buffet me everywhere I turn. I don't know French; the only thing I'm sure of is the word *rue*, which I suspect means "street." I am wearing a pair of flimsy pajamas and a silken robe, holding a slender cigarette holder. Somehow I feel as if I've been just thrown out of someone's home. No idea why; maybe it was something I'd said not of malice but got misinterpreted as such. Through the windows of crowded cafés, I see flappers and tuxedoed men laughing and carrying on, all having a good time. I see a reflection of myself in the window. I am frail and shivering, but no one inside ever notices. Maybe they're used to seeing higher-ups suddenly destitute the next day. Each polished round of cobblestone that I straggle across looks like daubs of paint. The glow of gaslight, heralding passengers from a Hector

Guimard–designed Art Nouveau entrance off the Paris Métro, is a halo looking for its angel.

Come to Paris. I'll find you.

Even though many of Djuna's friends read *Nightwood* and tittered among themselves when they figured out who was truly whom, it wasn't a runaway bestseller. She ended up having to ask for money from her friend Peggy Guggenheim when she moved into her tiny flat at 5 Patchin Place. There, she tried to write again, but drinking was much easier to do. The forties became a blur. Then she realized sometime in 1950 that she had to make a choice between liquor and art. Being an artist who had demanded impossibly much of herself to the point of drink, she made the more surprising choice. By redoubling her herculean efforts to write—and rewrite—her verse play *The Antiphon*, she had chosen art, a far more difficult and admirable addiction. Her family was not pleased to see themselves mocked so mercilessly onstage, but she'd stopped caring a long time before.

I've tried to read the play. I couldn't. It's dense, its language a brick wall. I'm never sure where it's going at times, and I don't feel emotionally engaged, but I like to think of it as Djuna's *Finnegans Wake*; that is, many people regard James Joyce's *Ulysses* as his masterpiece, and his final novel, *Finnegans Wake*, inscrutably so. The language of *The Antiphon*, if you stop trying to decode its overall plot in your first read, is dazzling, rich in cadence. Chloë and Veena have read the play a few times, and they "like" it, but only in the way that they're supposed to like it because scholars and critics have proclaimed it a masterpiece. No matter. If a writer can achieve something as singular and unique as *Nightwood* in spite of her mostly opaque output, she will always be remembered for the ages. *Nightwood* is a fevered dream unforgettable for the ages.

The pictures that Chloë and Veena emailed me from Paris depressed me in a way I hadn't expected. They had read a number of books about the Lost Generation, and the writers and artists who populated the Left Bank during the 1920s. They had done their first Djuna pilgrimage in New York when they got married twelve years before, and now they wanted to visit the many landmarks of the Left Bank.

When you hung up on me, they were due to leave for Paris the next day.

Two days later the pictures started coming, one after another, in my inbox. I recognized many of the landmarks from having seen pictures of Paris over the years, and I was naturally envious that they were over there, but I was more struck by the ordinariness of it all; not of the landmarks but of everything else around it. Tourists toting cameras were wearing all sorts of clothes: T-shirts, sneakers, and whatnot. A few even wore berets. They didn't seem to be thinking about style, or adhering to a sense of classic style that pervaded many pictures of Parisians some decades before. Then the cars. They were small and ordinary. No sense of identifiable style. Yet I couldn't pinpoint precisely why I'd felt so disappointed until I thought of color's power to transform.

Somehow everything becomes nostalgic when it's seen in black and white. Paris, even though it's supposed to be on the forefront of fashion and all, is the epitome of romantic nostalgia. Its landmarks have become shorthand for timelessness. Strip away its colors, and one begins to long for the one who got away. Such is the power of monochrome.

I've never taken a picture of you.

Never will I be able to correct my own memory of you against the reality of you on my iPhone's screen.

Memory is elastic, a rubber band, a roll of plastic wrap.

I will dream of you so much that you become taller, bigger, and broader only to shock me with your true dimensions when I see you again. The picture of you on Bear411 looks like it's about five years old; your beard had less gray.

It is said that our bodies undergo a full transformation every seven years.

Will I recognize you years from now, and will I still find myself with a dull ache burning that only you can heal? Will I be just like Djuna, who never had another great love after Thelma left her?

You were careful not to give me a memento of our times together. No physical traces of you, and yet my body plays you like a recording as if made yesterday.

Four months after you hung up, Chloë knocked sharply on my door. "We have come to ask you to tell me everything you know about the night . . ."

I rolled my eyes at the tone of her voice. It wasn't singsong; it was demanding as a mother's. Tired as I was, I had been sitting in front of my laptop, hoping to score a date online. Well, anything. Even a hookup would've been acceptable.

I put on my bathrobe and stepped out into the living room.

"Sit down," Chloë said in her best schoolteacher voice.

"What? What did I do?"

Chloë sat down next to Veena. "Honey, you want to start?"

"Bill, we're very, *very* worried about you."

"Well, it's just stuff at work."

"It's not work. I can tell. Was it that guy you used to see on weekends?"

I said nothing.

"Come on. You can trust us," Veena said. "What's his name?"

"He doesn't want anyone to know."

"Wait a minute. Let's guess—he's a closet case at risk of losing his trust fund if his parents found out about him?"

I chuckled. "No."

"Number two: he's a rising politician with a very dark past that he can't risk exposing because he's too in love with you and can't afford to lose you, but that's not how the movie ends in real life. He dumped you."

I looked at both of them, and I felt as if my tears were shooting bullets straight out of my eyes.

When they sat next to me with their arms around me, I blubbered out the story of us between swaths of Kleenex under my nose.

"How can I explain James to you?"

"That's the problem with gay guys. It's all about the look. You want to be seen with the hottest man in the bar so you can jack up your hotness quotient."

"He didn't . . ."

"Truly, I'm surprised. Haven't you learned anything from your Gender Studies degree?"

I explained how he didn't want me seen near him in public.

"What an asswipe."

I laughed. Veena had been lobbying everyone to stop using the word "asshole" and start using "asswipe." Chloë and I couldn't stop giggling whenever Veena used that word. "It's more colorful as we all need assholes, or we'd explode from so much shit inside us. Asswipe is a cleaner word."

God, it felt so good to laugh.

In that moment I realized that in our times together we've laughed uncontrollably only when we tickled each other that one time.

Had we been tiptoeing on eggshells around each other the whole time?

The thought saddened me.

It nevertheless felt good to start getting it off my chest. You were no longer a dirty secret.

I contemplated telling all my friends about you, but I wondered if they'd think I was making it all up because I was desperate for attention. No one would believe that a man as hot as you would want me because, after all, you didn't want to go anywhere in public with me. What did that say about me? Was I that grotesque?

Chloë picked up *Nightwood* and scanned its pages for a specific quote: "The lesson we learn is always by giving death and a sword to our lover. . . . take action in your heart and be careful whom you love—for a lover who dies, no matter how forgotten, will take somewhat of you to the grave."

James, was I good enough for a fuck, but not good enough to be seen with you in public?

Gee, thanks a lot. Even my cock should've seen that one coming a mile away.

Down on the escalator I stood with my purchase of underwear in the northern end of the Allston Mall, one of those sad affairs that never attracted a lot of high-end retailers, and up on the escalator coasted the curly-haired stranger I'd seen before. It was already summer, so he wasn't wearing his green parka. The sides of his head were trimmed, letting the curls on top of his head overflow a bit. He wore white-framed sunglasses and Converse sneakers. I didn't recognize him at all until he peered above his sunglasses and gave me a tiny smile that annoyed me so. Who the hell did he think he was? I thought of running down the escalator and jumping onto the other escalator so I could pursue him. He was a ghost made flesh; he existed, yet reappeared as if at will. It had been the first time I'd seen him after you hung up on me. Who was he, and what had he done to you? Ghosts are full of answers waiting for the right questions.

Over the weeks that followed, I told my housemates more about you in bits and pieces. It was sometimes hard to find the right words, and I'd always regarded myself as pretty articulate!

I felt like a ghost reporter when I recounted our times together. I left out the sexual details, of course, but I gave them the facts.

Veena hugged me now and then. "It's great that you're telling us so much."

Chloë was the one who'd said it best. "Losing Craig nearly killed you, and finding James brought you back from the dead. You can't let him kill you now."

Hearing it framed that way made a lot of things clear, but I wasn't satisfied. I wanted answers. I even asked Veena if I could use her phone to call you; not to talk with you, but to see whether you'd blocked my number. For a long time the telephone company said your number did not exist.

My heart beat louder than the ringing from your end.

You picked up. "Hello?"

I gave the phone back to Veena. "Sorry," she said. "Wrong number."

"Fuck. He's blocked me."

"Drop him. It's all about him. He's broken."

"Broken?"

"Yes, he's broken," Chloë said. "Forget about him."

"I don't understand. Broken?" I looked at her and Veena. "You talking about his foot?"

"No. His heart's been shattered into a million pieces, and he can't collect them all into his hands. He can't glue it all back together. Too hard, too painful. He's never going to heal. If what you say is true—that he's like the hottest stud around—he'll never have a shortage of guys who'll want to take care of him. That way he can stay broken and not do the heavy work on himself. As Djuna would say—" Veena reached for *Nightwood* and scanned the pages near the end. "I'm looking for this part where she says— oh! There it is: 'And why does Robin feel innocent? Every bed she leaves, without caring, fills her heart with peace and happiness. She has made her "escape" again.' Bill, I'm so, so sorry, but he really is broken."

I'd never thought that way about you.

Broken.

What a strange way to rethink you.

Almost insulting, even, when you consider how people had treated you differently because they saw your body as incomplete.

But broken?

I'd spent all this time believing that I was the damaged one. That you might be more broken than I am had never occurred to me.

I dreamed of being pushed along through a crowd screaming and hurling insults at me in a language I didn't understand. I didn't know what my crime was, only that I was full of stomach cramps. I couldn't stand to my full height without feeling the urge to keel over. It was probably botulism. I could not breathe normally, what with my swollen face, and my naked feet, which weren't toughened against razor pebbles, felt spikes of pain with each step. The rough-hewn rope scratched like knives around my neck; I was a starved dog being led to his execution. When I finally looked up, I saw that we were in a huge town square. Vultures waited expectantly in barren trees above the crowd; they appeared to be licking their beaks. Up ahead was the wooden platform. I couldn't wait to climb the steps for at least there wouldn't be such sharp teeth nipping at my feet. I felt myself zoning out until I bumped against the first step. Everything around me turned into a blur of noise and light and shadow. I pushed up on the steps, and as I did so, I felt slivers of wood poking at my bleeding feet. I wanted to scream out from the pain, but I was too parched to talk. Nonetheless I forced myself to lift one foot after another up the ten steps. I was not a suicidal person, but this I wanted: death.

A tall shadow crossed my face, and I tried to peer at it, shielding my eyes from the sun. He was tall and broad-shouldered like you, and his furry chest was scarred and tattooed with pagan icons. He had a gray burlap bag with holes cut out for his eyes over his head, and he had a huge ax in his hand. The ax swung ever so slightly, as if in anticipation of my raw neck. I called out your name, a whimper. He took the rope from my caretaker, and he pulled me sharply to let me know who was boss. There before me was a stump. I could see through many layers of old and dried blood the onion slice of years it had grown before it was chopped down. He pushed me down to my knees, which really hurt. He twisted my head to the side as the crowd's screams and insults turned louder and louder until I saw nothing but out of the corner of my eye the white bounce of light off his ax swinging high before severing my head. But the ax had been heavier than he'd expected, so it was a struggle to swing it upward; as he did so, the bag-mask fell off his head. It was me! The crime of you was so unforgivable that I had become my own executioner.

When Djuna first arrived in Paris, she didn't like the City of Light; she almost hated it for a few weeks. The French language and culture confused her, and everything else was strange, foreign. But when she began to meet other English-speaking expatriates all of the artistic bent, she felt more and more at home until she met Thelma Wood, a silverpoint artist. Ah, the lights of circus, the arcs of trapeze artist, the spectacles of white horses trotting in unison, the smell of sawdust and popcorn! Ah, Thelma! The very mistress of night herself had illuminated the darkness of day with gas-lit kisses. By then Djuna had been living in Paris for not even a year, and it wasn't long before the two women moved in together. They spent days and nights together at home and abroad, eventually amassing tender souvenirs that became a list, easily the most forlorn and the saddest, in *Nightwood*: "circus chairs, wooden horses bought from a ring of an old merry-go-round, Venetian chandeliers bought from the Flea Fair, stage-drops from Munich, cherubim from Vienna . . ." Each object, by its very mention, became invested with memory, fraught with emotion, until its power faded with the sun of years passing by. Why each object listed was important didn't matter; the very mention alone implied stories that only these two women would ever know. Each souvenir was chosen, born out of their own mythology. Djuna too surrendered these objects, but she clipped them all for the scrapbook of *Nightwood*.

I have no such mementos from our days and nights together; just memory, the most fragile of all gifts tendered between one human to another. The room of you is empty, but my bed is covered with musty trunks plastered with stickers of the countries I'd traveled with you. It is ready to collapse; there is too much weight. Memory, though light as air at first, turns heavy when not allowed to travel, gets lost. If worthwhile, it will come back; if not, perhaps it was not meant to be, already an insignificant detail not worthy of recall. What we do remember, of what we can when we are able to do so, says so much of what we'd valued back then. If that being the case, each orgasm we shared together is what had been important to me. Maybe trying to top our previous orgasm was so important that we found ourselves floundering in trying to braid the invisible yarns floating outward from our hearts to each other. We had so little experience in loving, truly loving, that when we had a chance, we flubbed it, not realizing what we'd just done until it was all over but the silence, the great silence that always shouts in our ears when we at last catch the sight of each other's shadow fading into the sunset. By then it will be too late to photograph what we'd seen in each other, and people younger than us will wonder what was such a big deal. Without scrapbooks of memory we are nothing.

AS WINDS BITTER AND CALM FLEE

If you think you can grasp me, think again:
my story flows in more than one direction
a delta springing from the river bed
with its five fingers spread.
                                        —*Adrienne Rich*

Oh, what of the night that makes us see the very things we are afraid of in broad daylight? What in the sinister detail keeps scratching at the edges of our eardrums that keep us from falling completely into the kind of sleep reserved for newborns? What of the gritty gravel spewed all over the smooth pavement so no rain can slip and slide wheels aside? What of the electrons blinking in blobs on the TV screen, leaking out windows where lonely men and women prowl the streets, never seeing each other as they pass? What of the wet cold that coats the grass blades like daggers, impaling the naked body of your dreams? What of the searing sip of scotch coursing down your throat, filling you aswirl with fire at a world gone mad? What of the distant eyes blinking blocks away before the car coasts closer to a stop, too late past the stripes of the pedestrian crossing? What of the crickets playing their locust song, needling the fireflies into staccato lightning until they too expire?

Oh oh oh, what of the night?

Answer me with the searchlight of your heart.

Tonight I'm feeling great. James, I haven't felt this great in a long time.

I think you'll be extremely upset to learn what happened to-night at the VFW Hall. I knew you wouldn't be there as it was a midweek night. My friends Ted and Steve wanted me to come play Drag Bingo with them, so why not play a dumb game for a change, right?

Well, guess who happened to sit next to me at the table?

A goateed guy with glasses. Thick curly hair. Rather slender. A confirmed Anglophile. Do you remember anyone like him? Quite a mysterious character.

No?

Let me refresh your memory: you called him a "nut" some months ago when I got into your truck one Friday evening.

Does that help?

All right: his name is Gordy Benjamin.

I'm sure you're rolling your eyes already.

I bet you'll think he has serious mental health issues.

Let's just say what he said about you was most enlightening. Most enlightening!

He had come in with a friend of his, and they happened to sit at our table. I introduced myself to them since—might as well, right? I did recognize him from before, so I didn't want to seem rude.

The game was fun with Lady Squirrelbutt calling out the num-bers. I didn't really care at all whether I won, and I didn't win at all. It was all for some charity.

I learned that Gordy was single.

I thought, Hm. Not exactly my type, but you know what? I'll give him a whirl. After all, Craig wasn't really my type, but we clicked anyway.

That's what I always have to remind myself when I meet some-one new. Give him a chance, like I gave Craig a chance, you know?

I asked Gordy how long ago was his relationship.

He said, "It ended last year."

His friend said, "He's still obsessed with James Sutton. Can you please help snap him out of it?"

I sat there slack-jawed.

Gordy gave me the queerest look. "I knew it!"

I whispered to him. "I'm tired of this game. Let's go outside for some air."

"Sure," he said. "I'm dying for a smoke."

Outside by the parking lot he offered me a cigarette, but I passed.

He really illuminated a lot of things. Truly.

Don't roll your eyes at me now.

You wanna know what he told me?

He said you were looking for a relationship when you met him at the Eagle thirteen years ago. You had lost your foot five years before.

He said your longest relationship had been six months.

He said you told him you always ended the relationship before the other guy did, so you wouldn't get hurt. "'Preemptive strike,'" he quoted you.

You should've seen the look on my face.

I thought Gordy was lying about you. I couldn't believe that you could be loquacious. What had happened to you between your time with Gordy and your time with me?

But that's not what interested me about Gordy.

He said you had a terrible problem that you wished no one should ever have. For a minute there I thought he'd meant your disability.

"Bill, didn't you hear what I said?"

"What?"

"That's why he broke up with you."

"I'm sorry. I'm not quite following you."

"He broke up with you because he was in love with you."

"What?"

"I know, I know. This sounds weird, but hear me out. He's totally incapable of using love and sex in the same sentence. The minute he falls in love with someone is the minute he loses sexual interest in him. Just like that."

Whoa, I thought. "Really? I've never heard of such a thing."

"It happens a lot more than you think. Sometimes there's such a thing as too much sex." He leaned closer to me. "My friend's wrong about me. I'm not obsessed with James. He knows that I've been dating a lot of guys these days, but he likes to needle me about James, the 'hottest man alive.' It's just annoying, but you know."

"He doesn't sound like much of a friend then."

"No, he's not, but he's proven himself useful now and then. Like now. He brought me to bingo when I wasn't in the mood to go out." He held out his hand and smiled. "Tonight I've made a new friend."

For the rest of the evening, we didn't talk about you at all. We talked about books and movies and music and theater. Oh, he's really a delightfully funny and smart guy. He works in marketing for the largest corporation in the city. You know the one I'm talking about. No wonder you'd broken up with him, and with so many others.

Including me. You *did* love me.

As I twist and turn, thinking of you, wondering how could I have been so oblivious, the foggy-eyed fool that I am, in my sleep toward dawn, I am cloaked with light, the same light as fireflies casting off the dust of day's sleep. I have no feet, yet I have no need of prosthetics. I am made of air, yet not of the dead and forgotten. Ahead are the weary streets of Paris, not of the 1920s, but right now, in the twenty-first century lit by LED bulbs and murmurs triangulated between cell phones constantly moving like blips on the radar screen, lined with tiny gas-efficient cars parked and still more moving along like cattle corralled toward their slaughter. This is not the Paris of Jean-Luc Godard's *Breathless* or even Jean-Pierre Jeunet's *Amélie*; this is the Paris of any other city in the world yet fortunately blessed with one jaw-dropping landmark after another. The night is blue-pearled with crescents of gold cascading across the older cobblestones not yet paved over. The striped awnings are painted with words in French that I don't know. I overhear snatches of conversation in French, Dutch, Korean, Polish, Japanese, German, and English between lovers and strangers looking at the glimmers of the Seine. It is frighteningly easy to travel anywhere in Paris; you just have to let your heart go and be there. Close your eyes and listen below you to the thousands and thousands of skeletons, the bones rearranged for ghoulish effect snaking along in the catacombs under the thick skin of the city. They whisper, sing; most of all they welcome you. They never get enough sparkling company, made more witty with the right amount of alcohol and cigarettes, showing up at the party. Right here, right now is Paris, not thousands of miles away, but right here in the cup of my hands holding the blood and tears of my heart. I can see my face in its mirror, and behind me are the clichéd lights of the Eiffel Tower. It's what tourists were trained to look for when they come here, and it's become shorthand for what Paris should be as no one has the time to understand anything more than what's there in the movies, but it's not the Paris I want to know and live in. The Paris I want to know has nothing to do with you, not that foreign language of you, for the Paris I had lived and breathed for too long, from Djuna from so long ago, has become a mausoleum, an art exhibit left in tatters after critics savaged all of it with their oil-hungry daggers. Djuna of the Storm King Mountain, who knew how far she'd travel from the days, ached for those happy years she spent with Thelma, and they took place, right there, on 173 Boulevard Saint-Germain and, later, 9 rue Saint-Romain, both on the Left Bank. She twisted and turned long enough to turn her hurt into spite, recasting horrors into *objets d'art*, the kind that would surely line the walls of the Louvre, a museum not of painted images but of words brutally sculpted as the Rodins. Victor Hugo and Arthur Rimbaud and Jacques Prévert and Jean Cocteau aren't the only gods of the page. The 1920s are dead like Ernest Hemingway and Gertrude Stein and Pablo Picasso and

Man Ray, and it's time that I seek a different kind of romance, the kind that will fill me with wist and wonder when I look back twenty, thirty years from now, with the kind of man who will look me in the eye and see the twinkle of stars, the same that Vincent van Gogh once daubed across the canvas stretched wide enough to embrace his startling visions and then some.

The twenty-first century, the known world no longer as vast and infinite, is right here, and I intend to live fully in the now. No matter where I am, I will create my own Paris. I will startle, for not to startle means a lifetime closer to death. I am a magician's cape filled with tricks, and I will captivate everyone I meet until you realize what a sleight of hand my heart was when you put your hand in your pocket only to find it empty. I am night, and my answers are full of day.

While you play again the game of love with someone else, the rest of us lonely men at the Eagle will eye you with hunger. We will nurse our drinks and make mindless chatter with each other not realizing how many of us have had a secret history with you. We will never talk about how much we wanted you, and we know it's not proper to wonder out loud about your prosthetic foot. We will one day form a brotherhood of men you didn't want to fuck after feeling those noodly strings tugging at your heart. We will compare notes on you, and before long, everyone else will know upfront the risks of loving you. Those of us still undeterred will feel the promise of hope because we imagine that if you're missing a foot, we will stand a chance with you. After all, we are physically complete even if we are not as dazzlingly gorgeous as you. We pray that you will want us to complete you, make you whole. That of course is utter bullshit, but that's why some people will gravitate toward people like you. They don't feel themselves complete, therefore they seek out others who are clearly broken.

Like I was.

I am far more complete than I'd ever realized, and it's got nothing to do with the fact that I have two feet. My soul inside me had felt like a ghost, and therefore I had to behave like one. I was ephemeral as a puff from your cigar, easily gone like ashes brushed off your fingers after a draw.

Others, unsuspecting, will come forth from the shadows to you. We will watch them try what we'd failed to achieve with you, and whisper among ourselves how much we'd tried, hoped. We don't need to say much. If we can't be part of the bear community, I suspect that we'd be content with knowing we weren't alone in loving you. You like to sit and model. Sometimes you will unbutton your shirt, or take it off. If you've got the fur, you might as well flaunt it. We'd be something like the First Ex-Wives Club, except that you've never proposed to any of us; Gordy has joked that we should call ourselves the Sutton-Dumped Club. Those of us whose hearts you've broken will observe others, not yet knowing your history, melting in your presence. A few of them may feel cheeky enough to approach you with a hello.

It's a game that you play only to lose. You must like it that way because why else do you keep playing it?

Do you want to know what else Gordy's told me about you? He eventually met others who were involved with you over the years, so he pieced together what he thinks is your story.

Your father was a major alcoholic who'd managed to hold down his job as schoolteacher right up until the day he retired. You left home as soon as you could, and you never came back. You had five brothers and sisters, and you'd changed your name once your daughter came of age so your ex-wife couldn't track you down. That would explain why Annie would've appeared out of nowhere after so many years. Not sure if I believe this part. Sutton is not an ethnic name like so many others—Finns, Swedes, Norwegians—up north where you grew up.

Your mother couldn't deal with the emotional travail of raising six kids and the strain of keeping your father at bay. You saw him hit her repeatedly when she insisted that he hit her instead of the kids. She spent her days recovering from the bruises, and she needed to be left alone. She couldn't bear to be touched by anyone.

No wonder you didn't keep beer in the fridge, and no wonder you didn't want me to cuddle you all night long.

Gordy believes you'd learned from your parents that love invited only emotional and physical pain, so you couldn't bear the potential hurt of love. What then now? Should I punch you on the jaw because that was all you'd learned of love? Should I demand that you never be touched because you were only worthy as a punching bag? Should I denigrate you and call you all sorts of names so you'd know how much I loved you? What is *love* to you?

Then Gordy told me a story about you that shocked me. Some guy named Charlie, who was a struggling potter, gave you a box of cheap cigars for your birthday. You insisted he return it for better quality cigars, which he couldn't afford. Charlie felt like crap because he'd let you down. If this story is indeed true, you should be ashamed of yourself for not appreciating the intent of his gesture. Doesn't matter if the gift wasn't up to your standards. Someone took the time to think of you long enough to get you something, even though he was quite broke. You say thank you, and just smoke it! Don't be so selfish, okay?

Gordy told me another story from someone else named David. You were quite the hiker before the accident. This I hadn't fully realized about you, but I should've known from the way you were able to scale that hill near your house. It wasn't just your height or the way you walked; you were made for slope and altitude. David, the guy you were seeing at the time, had been thin all his life so he'd never felt the need to work out. He had such high metabolism that he could eat anything and not gain a pound. One week you and David went out west to somewhere in Idaho. David did warn you that even though he had some camping experience growing up, he didn't have much hiking experience, but he was game to try. You moved so quickly up the mountain that every time you paused, you were seething from impatience at what you'd perceived as David's slowness. You didn't have trouble breathing at the higher altitudes, but he wasn't used to it. You lashed out at him because he was keeping you behind in your goal of covering a certain distance each day. David was shocked. He'd thought that the two of you would share a week of communing with nature, but you didn't seem to care about accommodating him. David turned around and went down. He left you standing there, and you were quite incensed by the time you two returned to the parking lot. David said absolutely nothing, wouldn't say anything to your face, demanded to use the telephone in the ranger's office to change his plane ticket while the park ranger gave you a what-the-hell-is-going-on look, went outside and found a ride back to town with two day-trippers returning from the mountains, taxied to the airport back home. He was sorry at first to learn of your accident, but he later became happy when he realized that maybe your disability would teach you to be more patient with others.

Gordy told me many more stories from men you'd discarded. I was truly astonished. I had no idea that you'd become an anthology of selfishness. The problem with physical beauty is that people in awe of it will excuse a lot of ill behavior. Thanks to you, I've become grateful that I was never so beautiful I'd forget how to treat others with kindness and compassion.

Love—if that was loosely what we had—had to be on *your* terms only. That's not love. That's possession. When you felt you couldn't control the relationship, you had to end it. No wonder we lasted only six months.

I hadn't seen that one coming, but it seems so obvious now.

Of course, you didn't want me to meet any of your friends or be seen in public with me or meet my housemates, because if that happened, you'd lose control over our relationship. You just can't discard people for no reason at all. Just not right.

Not long after I met Gordy, we went to see a play called *Plum da Faeries* at the Punkhead. It was an outrageous take on Shakespeare's *A Midsummer Night's Dream*, except that they were all Mafioso fairies who liked to cross-dress while drinking one martini after another one long night in a penthouse. It was funny!

When we joined the audience filing out of the theater, I noticed Matt sitting in his wheelchair by the entrance. I hadn't made the connection between him and the director's name—Matthew J. Madden—in the program notes until that moment.

"Excuse me," I said to Gordy.

The crowd had thinned enough that he could see me coming. I was afraid that he'd roll away, but he didn't. He gazed at me as if he had nothing to hide, and he was right. *I* had been hiding too much.

"Hi, I just wanted to tell you how much I enjoyed your play, it was funny as all get out, I'm so fucking sorry for being such an asshole weeks ago, I still have your number taped to the wall above my desk, I was a jerk, I should've—"

"Stop." He held up his hand. "It's okay."

"You scared me because you were so strong."

"Right. Crips are supposed to be weak."

I slowly shook my head. "Well, I felt like anything I said or did would make you make me feel like crap, when I was trying my damn best to understand you. I hate the feeling that my best is never going to be good enough for you. Ever."

"No, that's not true," he whispered. "You know that's not true."

"Then stop knocking me down all the time. I'm not every able-bodied person who's given you the middle finger, so just stop taking it out on me, okay? I fucked up, okay, and I'm sorry. Okay?" I glanced back at Gordy. "I gotta go."

"Are you going to call me?"

"Maybe." I couldn't look into his eyes. "I don't know."

Would I date a disabled man again? You bet your ass I would, but not if he felt unable to mix love and sex in the same sentence. I deserve someone who is fluently bilingual in love *and* sex. Just not you.

I looked at Matt's number on the wall above my dresser. What the hell. I picked up my phone and dialed. "Hey?"

"Who's this?"

"Bill Badamore. This is Matt, right?"

"Oh, yeah." A brief pause. "I thought you'd never call."

"I've decided that giving you the silent treatment wasn't fair to you."

He laughed. "Oh, it's okay, bud. How are you doing?"

We met again, and this time we had burgers and fries at Beefy Guys. We had a great time. I think he'd figured that he should lay off on disability politics and hang loose with me. I didn't think I'd feel so relaxed with him, but I did.

Did I end up having sex with him? No. Did I want to? You betcha. He's solid. His thick arms and toughened fingers remind me of this important fact. Just like yours did.

I admit to worrying about the logistics of sex with someone who can't stand on his knees like you can, but you know what? Try I must, but I'm not going to worry about it. All I hope is that he'll invite me up to his place, and soon.

There in the distance, as the cobblestones gleamed in the street-lamps of Paris, I espy two slender women with tight-fitting hats and dark capes swinging just so above their clackety heels. I know instantly who they are.

Djuna and her beloved Thelma.

I gaze upon Thelma's face. She was the face of love itself. No wonder she had been the love of Djuna's life; not just her, but a few others, too.

Thelma smiles, almost a coquette, and huddles closer to her.

Djuna smiles demurely as she takes out a silver-encrusted lighter from inside her cape and flicks it to light her brown cigarette. A different aroma, a different smoke tickles in the insides of my nose. I want to sneeze, but I don't. She has come from a time different from mine.

She is night itself. She has come to inject me with the narcotic of night. Thelma gleams confidently as day. She's not the candle of confusion that burned lives through the pages of *Nightwood*.

Djuna pulls out a cigar from inside my jacket. I am surprised that it was there.

She tears off one end of the cigar and holds it up to me.

I lean forward to accept it in my mouth.

"May I?" she asks.

I nod assent.

She lights my cigar. Thelma weaves her arm into Djuna's, and they fade into black.

Meanwhile my head mushrooms inside with memories, a haze of smoke and sweetness. I am awash in dreams thick as molasses. Yes, I would write the story of us. I'd change your name and your disability. Our story would be a *roman à clef* like *Nightwood*. Let the world play the guessing game of who's who in its pages. I too would become highfalutin with my writing: if I belly-flopped at verse, I shall soar in my prose. Each sentence would be rethought with the muscles of language turning me into a new contortionist of the tongue. I will work out with the weight of words so well that I can lift a thousand pounds with my pinkie finger, toss it up like a baton, and file my nails while I await its lofty return. I wouldn't be afraid of waxing poetic with descriptions of how we met and being nonlinear with the plot. I would take risks whenever I could, just to see if I could fly. I am both owl and mouse. Above all I would strive for art and be the artist I was long afraid to become. I'd make Djuna proud of me. Or maybe not, as she's ether now. I wouldn't dare imitate Djuna—no one could. It took her forty-four years to master the language of night before she felt strong enough to turn on the light bulb in the operating room of night. But I would honor her spirit, the very night of fog that had made her name. I have been a soul talking to myself in the heart of night, and it's time that someone else listen. I would write of the shadow that was you, and it would be so well-written everyone would believe that my fiction is truth. I am an art historian. I will document the provenance of you, the greatest masterpiece I have ever had the pleasure of studying. My book would become the lecture no one cares to attend until they see you in the flesh and fill with wonder. That face. That chest. That cock. That missing foot. You will turn each man who shares your bed into a detective, and they shall consult for clues. We men may share the same anatomy, and yet we find novelty in the variations in our bodies. That is the difference between us and the ghosts that haunt our lives. We both are different and living, and the ghosts are all one and the same. Let them all float away.

When I woke up this morning, the opening gambit was clear as day: "Your missing right foot was only a part of you, just like the fur that blanketed your body . . ."

I will pull back the curtain of shame and reveal all of you, including your missing foot. I will not hide that of you. I will display on your face the pride of being different from everyone else. I will not make you a saint or a villain. You just are.

I will render the details of your body so clearly that people unaccustomed to seeing raw sensuality will have to avert their eyes and accuse me of obscenity when you were merely standing there. Not even an erection. They will wish that you'd trim your mountainous pubic hair, that you should shave your chest so you can be smooth like a woman, that you'd just button up your shirt and hide the one thing everyone always zeroes on when they see a man naked.

I wonder how they'd react if you lifted your right leg up like an erection. Would they be repelled by the contours of your amputation, or would they still turn away and look at your cock instead, pretending not to have seen the very thing that was supposed to differentiate you from them? What you have left of your body is a gift. When you walk out in the world, you challenge them to consider the possibility that they too could end up like you. The fear is so great that they have to turn away from you. The ones who don't are the ones you want to be friends with. They are the ones who get that you're more than an amputee.

When you stand there like a giant up in the clouds of my dreams, partially lit by a raging fire, I fret that I'll never be able to capture your mercury nature with my brushstrokes. You are so epic that I can't just be Georges Seurat, applying tiny gobs of paint so patiently and placing them next to similar gobs of different colors to achieve a whole new color when viewed from the distance. Trying to paint you would be dizzying, like trying to take in a newspaper-dotted Chuck Close image up close while trying to connect the dots. I'd need to take many steps far back and absorb the big picture of you.

I feel so helpless when I wonder how I'll ever measure up to the masterpiece that is you, but paint I must.

Start anywhere. The road I've taken has already gone past your house.

On the first day of winter, the warmth of summer had arrived.

In high school Matthew used to be a gymnast. He knew his way around the bars and beams, and he wasn't afraid of velocity and gravity when he spun high up in the air. His sense of balance was perfect. Training was demanding, but he derived great pleasure out of aiming for grace in the air. Not a wasted movement, and all clocked to a single song. Just was. A blur, a moment of suspense, the stark realization of this is all it's going to come down to. His tights were buff and blue, the high school colors, and he photographed well with his medals and trophies.

Then one morning he had a stroke just before he was to start another day of classes. The part of his brain that regulated his leg movements went dead. He woke up in a hospital room, confused, groggy, frightened, not realizing that a few days had passed. Then they told him: "We need to work your legs."

But those muscular legs, the pride and joy of his existence, the way he executed his straight legs like scissors opening so precisely in air and while swinging between parallel bars did not want to work, wouldn't work, couldn't, can't. He was seventeen years old, and his dreams of competing in the Olympics died with his legs. It was odd not to feel anything in his legs; they had essentially gone numb, and he couldn't feel pain or warmth. He had to learn how to keep his legs warm even if he didn't feel anything. He still needed physical therapy to exercise his legs to prevent atrophy. He was grateful, though, that he could still get hard, so that was good.

He hated sitting in his wheelchair, quite humiliating during his last year of high school, he had never hated the word "sorry" as much as he had in those days, so he fell into the habit of watching movies as a way of keeping his mind off things. That was how he decided to become a director. He didn't know of any disabled directors then, but his former coach encouraged him not to worry. He went to Browell University, which he wasn't crazy about as they kept giving him less interesting plays to direct, but in hindsight he was grateful. The so-called boring plays required him to make the direction more dynamic, more compelling. He had to look for fresh takes on the classics. He had to study actors on stage, and in rehearsal. The entire process was really no different from training for a competition, except that it wasn't just one person swinging up in the air. A small army had to be there to catch each actor should she fall. He grew to love the theater, couldn't stop reading stage plays, watching TV programs and movies on DVD, and he couldn't imagine being away from watching the stage. He was helping to tell stories. More powerful than just another Yurchenko.

Matt is not a ghost. His spirit is of the flesh. The sex we have is not as blindingly intense as you and I had, but it is far richer, more lasting, and more emotional in a good way. We laugh, and we smile, and we hold hands. This is what genuine intimacy is about. He's let me in, and his heart is an amazing ocean. When he kisses me, I feel the sky.

Unlike you, he loves to talk yet loves to listen. His observations are at times so profound that I simply have to hold his hand and kiss him. In that sense I've become just like Craig. I finally understood how he'd felt about loving me because at the time he overwhelmed me. I was sometimes annoyed by his PDA. I hope to annoy Matt with my PDA.

You see, when I met you, I'd forgotten I was worthy of reciprocation.

Hello guys!

Time to update my profile. I've met the most amazing man. He's the guy on my left in the first three pictures. I'm very happily off the market. Asking him out for a second date was the smartest thing I've ever done. He's a total badass.

Some have asked me how I was able to find such a hunky boyfriend.

Wanna find the man of your dreams? Just close your eyes and listen to your heart. He may not look like the stud you've always wanted, but he may feel the same way about you. Just close your eyes and stop judging each other on the basis of looks, cock size, etc. You can't have selfishness in a relationship for it to work.

I saw this on my friend's profile (hi Norm2231!): "You wanna have the best sex/orgasm ever? Try it with someone you love. All the sex in the world won't fill an empty heart."

Looking forward to hearing from ya.

Thanks for reading, guys!

Bill

LAST UPDATED ON OCT 11, 2014

When I did see you again, it was at the OctoBear Dance a year after you and I met. Matt and I were there to meet up with some friends of ours who were entertaining guests from New York. You sat by yourself at a table by the dance floor, and you looked the same in your baseball cap, flannel shirt, and jeans.

This time I wasn't hoping for you to kiss me again. I was too busy feeling shy with Matt's hand holding mine. I was still skittish with the idea of loving someone who was emotionally available. How could I have been so lucky? It's truly astonishing how afraid people are of loving others who are different from them, and how easy it is to love when you listen to only each other's heart.

When the DJ switched over to Moby's ethereal ballad "I'm Not Worried at All," Matt pulled me onto the floor for a slow dance. I knelt before him and closed my eyes as I rested my head on his shoulder. He wasn't as tall or beefy as you, and he had never cared for wearing flannel shirts, but I didn't care anymore about any of that. I had to stop rejecting people on the basis of their looks. So many of us are born with bodies we don't want because society is always telling us that we need better bodies. Period. This way corporations can make money off our insecurities. The only security they can bank on is our deep sense of insecurity. What mattered was that Matt wanted to hold me in public. Unlike you, he wasn't ashamed of being seen with me in public.

The song ended.

You were gone.

I smiled at Matt.

"What's so funny?"

"I'll tell you later. You'll read about it."

Funny thing was, I had never told Matt about you; I didn't want to. I didn't want the toxin of you to poison Matt and me. Besides, we had better things to talk about.

Through the feverish act of writing the story of us, I had exorcised the ghost of you from my body. In my heart, it's always summer.

Are there things of the day here in the room of night? Do they shimmer like glowworms? Or do they sigh and give off the faintest light? Day is the forbidden creature of night; it is a foghorn of clarity and happiness against the fog of obfuscation and obsolescence. It is the worst kind of drug; once tasted, the addiction is impossible to break. Day is heat, fire, love. It is a dog curled up next to your feet, contented that you are nearby and not going anywhere. Day is the powder of fingerprints difficult to remove; once touched, we turn instantly into hooligans. We want to break into houses of dark moods and swing anchors of death through the window so the zeppelins can let go and float stately like the ships that they are. Our eyes are bright as flashlights sweeping like spotlights, showing the rigor mortis of dead objects no longer dusted with meaning. History has been erased from their skins. No archeologist will ever be able to decode its many mysteries. The walls of Pompeii need to be cleared of ash, its stories overlapping each other until they echo songs freed of history. If night be ghost, then day must be angel. Fly, fireflies, fly and startle.

This dream shall not be dreamed again.

Years later at the Eagle, a buddy of yours will take you aside and point at me while I'm standing with Matt by the bar. I'll probably wear a favorite T-shirt, the latest being CAREFUL, OR YOU'LL END UP IN MY NOVEL. "You know that guy with glasses standing next to the guy in the wheelchair? That's Bill Badamore. He wrote this *interesting* book . . . wait, what was the title again? Oh, right: *Flannelwood.* Anyway, it's about a disabled bear. Have you ever heard of it?"

You will shake your head no, but you'll search online for my book later that night and order a copy. The hot daddy bear on the cover looks suspiciously just like you.

In the darkness of your den with your lonely lamp peering over your shoulder, you'll find my nonlinear writing not your style. You'll think that my story was fancy-schmancy hooey with a lot of unnecessary poetic asides. You'd roll your eyes at how I'd changed details of our relationship and your disability; how much of you I'd gotten wrong yet how much more of you I'd gotten right. As you know, I've even changed the geography of the city where we met; I made it rather generic, a city almost anywhere in the Midwest. All of this may be a work of fiction, but my heart has never lied.

When you're at last done with *Flannelwood*, you will take off your reading glasses and weep with only the rickety arms of darkness comforting you in that windchill of lonesomeness. No one has ever written a book about you, just for you. Here is this book with your initials at the very end, on its last page: "for J.A.S."

It's my epitaph for the lichen-covered tombstone honoring our memory. You are love's tree gone hollow, an elegy.

Of course, James, you'll never tell me any of the above because you'd know just then what a damn fool you were to hang up on me in the first place. This you will mourn until the end of your days, and this you will remember with each puff of cigar you exhale with the latest weekend trick. Nothing will ever be the same.

I am paper. Crumple me up and throw me into the fireplace, but I will never fade into embers. I'm a brick.

I am not a cigar stub you can toss away. I will burn so brightly long into the night that I become an everlasting day. I am the diamond that illuminates each snowflake from within.

Too much pride can be a disability, you know. A little humility may be your best course of rehabilitation.

Love is hard, but it doesn't have to be a country song. You can start by calling your daughter Annie and ask for forgiveness. Welcome her back into your life. You're a grandfather now. Absence does not love make. Think about that.

Start anywhere, and there you are.

All it takes is one phone call.

Really.

By then I'll have long hung up on you and married Matt.

And, oh, what of the night? I think you already know the answer.

for J.A.S.

BIOGRAPHICAL NOTE

Raymond Luczak is the author and editor of twenty-two books. Titles include *The Kinda Fella I Am: Stories* and *QDA: A Queer Disability Anthology*. His Deaf gay novel *Men with Their Hands* won first place in the Project: QueerLit Contest 2006. His work has been nominated ten times for the Pushcart Prize. He lives in Minneapolis, Minnesota. He can be found online at raymondluczak.com.